UNSUCCESSFUL

FAILURE AND SUCCESS ARE TWO SIDES OF SAME COIN, TOSS IT.

UNSUCCESSFUL

SANDEEP S. KASHYAP

White Falcon
Publishing

Unsuccessful
Sandeep S. Kashyap

Published by White Falcon Publishing
Chandigarh, India

The contents of this book have been certified and timestamped
on the Gnosis blockchain as a permanent proof of existence.
Scan the QR code or visit the URL given on the back cover
to verify the blockchain certification for this book.

ISBN - 978-81-19510-33-7

"Success is never accidental,
And accidental success never lasts longer."

Message from Neena Kulkarni

Dear Sandeep,

As I turn the final page of the transcript of your book 'Unsuccessful, I am left deeply moved by your story. Yours is a journey of relentless discoveries, self-search, curiosity, insights, struggles and gains. That you excel as a creative writer is evident from the absolutely mesmerising descriptions of some of your experiences. The Shantaram episode is indeed fascinating, as is the bat collecting one. You describe with such elan and detail, that the entire scenario plays before the readers eyes!

I particularly appreciate the warning notes you offer to young aspirants stepping into the world of filmmaking and advertising. Your novel should become a handbook for them to refer to.

Your ability to be objective about yourself is another aspect which I must mention. Not every writer is honest enough to see where he/she have failed, or have gone astray, and, moreover, to admit it, and correct the mistakes the second time round.

You call yourself Unsuccessful after gaining so much in experience and adventure, knowledge and creativity? You have the greatest riches and valuables in the form of sheer experience in your field, and the generosity to share them with the world!

I wish you all the success in your endeavours. May good health and creative imagination be your constant companions.

In admiration,

Neena Kulkarni.

CONTENTS

PROLOGUE

During a recent lecture at a media school in Mumbai, I posed a simple question to the attentive students seated before me: "Why have you chosen this particular path of education for your future career?" To my surprise, not a single student, out of the seventy present, could provide a truly satisfying answer. Responses such as "This was my only option due to lower scores in twelfth grade," "I joined because my friends were enrolling in this media school," or "I love films," echoed through the room. One over-smart kid said "I want to replace Shah Rukh Khan." I admired his guts but at the same time felt pity for his overconfident attitude. Not a single student articulated their ambition as, "Filmmaking is my passion, and I aspire to become a skilled filmmaker." Many seemed oblivious to the array of challenging sub-streams within filmmaking, such as Scripting, Art Direction, Costume Designing, Makeup Artistry, Production Control, and more, beyond the conventional realms of Acting and Directing. I am not suggesting that the picture is identical in all media schools, but it is generally quite similar across the board.

It was disheartening to realise that these budding talents lacked a clear vision of their post-graduation pursuits. While their passion burned brightly, the absence of a roadmap ahead spurred me to embark on documenting my own filmmaking journey in the form of a book.

The impulse to document my reflections at this stage of life emerged instinctively. Upon retrospection, I find myself astounded by the trajectory I've traversed—a journey veering towards a nebulous future goal. Circumstances and surroundings nudged me in its direction, albeit initially hazy and indistinct. I drifted, searching for clarity amidst the haze, a quest that stretched across time.

Ultimately, as I honed in on my destination, it dawned upon me: perhaps I arrived a tad late. Yet, the mantra "Better late than never" echoed in my mind, propelling me forward. Subsequently, I grasped a vital truth—that in life, punctuality to one's purpose is paramount. Otherwise, the desired outcome remains elusive. More than everything I feel success and failure are two sides of the film making coin. We have to toss it high up; the result will be decided by our hard efforts and destiny.

Through this endeavour, I aim to shed light on motivational axioms that falter in practicality. For instance, the oft-repeated adage "Learn from your mistakes" holds merit. I advocate a more pragmatic approach: Learn from others' mistakes.

This book serves as an earnest confession—of an unfiltered account of my journey towards success, riddled with the detours of perfectionism, culminating in the stark realisation of my identity as a filmmaker. I will call it 'Unsuccessful'.

I agree that success or failure is a subjective concept, varying from person to person. While I am content with my accomplishments thus far, I do believe that with proper guidance in my formative years, the outcome might have been different.

In my journey, I hold no intention of harming or disparaging those who have crossed my path. Instead, I have chosen to absorb the positivity they have offered and release any negativity, allowing only the good aspects to shape my life.

Sandeep Kashyap

1

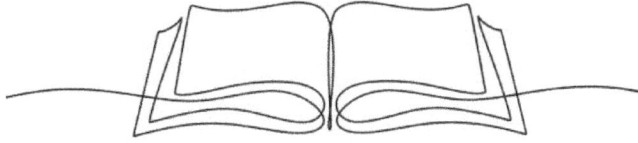

BEGINNING

In today's world, parents often strive to instil passion and ambition in their young ones through various means. While this approach to grooming our children is not necessarily wrong, it is crucial to recognise that passion and ambition are intrinsic qualities that cannot be manufactured. Particularly in the formative years of childhood, when young minds are still tender and impressionable, children may not be fully cognisant of the myriad opportunities that lie before them. Therefore, it becomes essential to expose them to a wide range of avenues and possibilities, guiding them gently towards self-discovery and personal growth. However, it is important to tread carefully, as coercing or pressuring children into pursuing paths solely for material gain can lead to potential disaster in the long run.

In the past, the scope of education was often limited to three primary streams: becoming a doctor, an engineer, or a lawyer. There was a pervasive lack of awareness regarding alternative career paths, with fields such as acting, filmmaking, and theatre being disparaged as inferior options. Even today, many parents continue to hold onto the perception that pursuing a career in film is a fallback for those who cannot succeed in traditional academic pursuits. While this may sound like a bold assertion to the younger generation, it reflects a prevailing reality that has persisted over time.

My father's words of wisdom have always resonated with me: "If you choose to stitch boots, strive to master it just like Bata." This advice underscores the importance of wholeheartedly dedicating oneself to any chosen profession or craft, emphasising the value of excellence and expertise regardless of the field.

From my earliest years, I nurtured a deep-seated passion for exploring the silver screen. While my peers revelled in outdoor activities and games, my heart was captivated by the enchanting cinema and theatre. Creativity ran in my family's blood; my mother, a renowned Hindustani classical singer, possessed a deep love for the stage. She was also a film buff in her early age. Watching a film first day first show was like a routine for her in her college days. She even graced productions of The Goa Hindu Association, a well-respected theatre group in Mumbai during the 1950s. However, as the group transitioned from amateur to professional productions, the perceived lack of dignity associated with the arts compelled her to bid this passion farewell. This narrative underscores the societal attitudes of that era, where pursuits in the arts were often undervalued and deemed less respectable than traditional professions.

In the year 1956, amidst the prevalent joint family culture, my parents tied the knot. My father's side resided in an ancestral home located on Gowalia Tank Road in Mumbai, while my mother's family owned two buildings in the Grant Road area. This marital union not only bridged two distinct family backgrounds but also brought together diverse residential settings, reflecting the varied social strata of Mumbai during that time.

While it may seem like the beginning of a personal biography, delving into this background is crucial before delving into my path towards filmmaking. The decision of my parents to move to Goa during that era holds significant weight, as it has the potential to alter the trajectory of my life entirely. Had they chosen to remain in Mumbai, my life's course would have unfolded in a manner starkly different from the path I eventually embarked upon in later years.

My father chose to work as a manager at a private powerhouse owned by my maternal grandfather in 1961. My mother hailed from a notably affluent family during that era, with extensive properties in Goa, including iron ore mines, diverse factories and mills, as well as two towering five-storey structures in Grant Road.

This powerhouse was one among them located in the quaint village of Curchorem, Goa. His position as Manager held a revered status in our community. His pivotal role in supplying electricity, particularly during the nascent years of Goa's liberation from Portuguese rule (1961-65), bestowed upon him a princely aura within our village.

Leaving our residence in Mumbai, situated in our ancestral house at Crown Mansion in Gowalia Tank located in South Mumbai was according to me, a move he made in haste. I am not blaming him for that, but his future was more secure in Mumbai and not in Goa.

Our abode was a big one, accommodating a large joint family comprising my grandmother, my uncle and his wife, my parents, and my father's five sisters. The untimely demise of my grandfather, when my father was merely eight years old, imposed a significant responsibility on my father and uncle, who toiled relentlessly to acquire and upkeep this extensive property in Mumbai. Perhaps due to this circumstance, he may have considered relocating from Mumbai to Goa.

Reflecting on the past, the prospect of remaining in Mumbai sparks contemplation about how vastly distinct my life trajectory might have been. However, as life inexorably unfolds, it becomes evident that destiny holds sway over our paths, guiding us through unforeseen turns and shaping the course of our existence.

Amidst this backdrop of picturesque Goa, our entire fast-paced lifestyle of Mumbai changed to laid-back attitude of Goa. "Sushegad" is what they call it in Portuguese.

My passion actually developed during this time when I was just four years old. I never knew what passion was, but in later years, I understood-

Feeling super, super happy and excited about something you really like to do or learn about. That super happy feeling is called passion! It's like when you find something that makes you really happy and you want to keep doing it because it feels so good inside.

I enjoyed unrestricted access to the village's only cinema hall, Cine Niagara. From the tender age of four, I embarked on my cinematic journey, initially accompanied by my parents and later, under the tutelage of an attendant who shared my obsession for film. Though the powerhouse eventually transitioned into government hands in 1966, my ardour for cinema endured. I forged relationships with the cinema hall's staff— manager, doorkeepers, and projectionist—who facilitated my continued cinematic odyssey.

In the quaint serenity of our humble abode in a sleepy town in Goa, a pivotal moment unfolded that would etch itself into the life's mosaic of my very being, igniting a flame of passion within me that would come to define my existence. At tender age of twelve, an encounter transpired that would alter the course of my life forever, casting me into the enchanting realm of filmmaking.

It all began with a gesture as grand as the silver screen itself - the only cinema hall in town graciously extended to us complimentary seats for the premiere's final show, a gesture that whispered promises of untold adventures and captivating tales waiting to be told. The allure of those flickering images on the big screen sparked a yearning within me, a yearning to weave my own narratives with light and shadow, and to capture the essence of life's myriad stories.

As twilight draped its comforting shroud upon our veranda, casting a spell of tranquillity upon us, a figure materialised, bearing the name Shantaram Joshi from the mystic lands of Satara, Maharashtra. Holding a small harmonium wrapped in cloth. Clad in the simplicity of a kurta and pyjama, his presence exuded an enigmatic charm that captivated my impressionable soul. His eyes, beheld through lenses akin to bulky paperweights, gleamed with a blend of mystery and wisdom, reflecting a world unseen and unexplored.

"What do you want me to do?" My father's enquiry cut through the stillness of the evening, his voice laced with curiosity and a hint of apprehension. Shantaram, initially reserved, began to speak with a gentle politeness that commanded attention.

"I narrate cinema like a one-man show. I hold within me the essence of about a hundred and fifty Hindi and Marathi films, each a detailed story waiting to be unveiled like a practical cinema experience", Shantaram uttered, retrieving the worn notebook from his cotton bag full of notebooks, one extra pair of clothes, and a thin towel. He shared it with my father.

"Someone in the village guided me to seek your aid, as they deemed you the sole beacon of hope in my quest. I am unable to partake in physical toil due to ailing health, and this gift of narration is my only sustenance," his words carried the weight of both desperation and determination.

Perusing the notebook, my father observed the testimonials of esteemed individuals who had borne witness to Shantaram's artistry, their praise illuminating the faded pages with a glow of reverence. "There is nothing immediate that I can offer, but grant me until tomorrow. In the interim..." my father's voice trailed off as he contemplated how to assist this enigmatic stranger.

"...In the meantime, I will find solace elsewhere," Shantaram's admission carried a touch of vulnerability, offering a glimpse into his reliance on the kindness of others.

"Do not fret. Our veranda has ample space. You shall stay with us," my father's proclamation echoed with a sense of unwavering generosity, his gaze shifting to my mother as he instructed her to include Shantaram in our evening repast. My mother, her demeanour a portrait of silent understanding, wordlessly assented, as if she had foreseen this exchange long before it took place. At that moment, beneath the starlit sky and the melody of rain outside, a silent pact of compassion and camaraderie was forged, binding our fates together in a tapestry of unforeseen connections.

On the very next day, with just a single nod from my father, the announcement of Shantaram's show echoed through the village like a whisper in the wind. Word swiftly spread, carried on the breath of anticipation, drawing folks from far and wide to the courtyard of the Mahadev temple. As the clock struck eight in the evening, a tale of its own unfolded.

What was initially anticipated to be a modest gathering of forty to fifty souls blossomed into a vibrant congregation of over a hundred eager spectators, each crafting their own cosy nook on the temple floor. Surprised by the surge in attendance, my father sprang into action, swiftly orchestrating the arrangement of a microphone and speakers to ensure every whispered word and hushed sigh found its way to the hearts of the enchanted audience.

As the night descended upon the temple courtyard, a hushed anticipation hung heavy in the air, like an invisible veil of intrigue. With a mere flicker of his hand, Shantaram conjured the time-honoured ritual of a cinematic overture, mimicking the familiar hum of a film projector with uncanny precision. The audience, enraptured by this ingenious prelude, found themselves transported into the realm of celluloid magic.

With a voice that resonated with the authority of a seasoned showman, Shantaram delved into the minutiae of the censor certificate, unfurling the arcane details of its issuance date, the film's length measured in reels, and every intricate specification in between. The meticulous care with which he recounted each detail painted a tapestry of authenticity, setting the stage for the grand tapestry of storytelling about to unfold.

As a melody danced from the keys of a small harmonium, weaving a symphony of anticipation, the logo of the production house materialised before the audience's eyes, its presence a herald of the cinematic voyage about to ensue. Shantaram's hands, swift and sure, caressed the harmonium with practiced ease, coaxing forth the strains of the title music that peppered the air with a melodic allure.

In a flurry of movement and a cascade of words, he breathed life into the main credits, each name resonating like a sonnet of praise in the audience's ears. The main actors, the visionary director, the maestro behind the music, the eyes of the cinematographer capturing unseen worlds, and the deft hands of the editor sculpting narratives—each introduction was a crescendo of anticipation, a prelude to the epic saga waiting to be unfurled. This initial enchantment wove a spell so potent, so utterly captivating, that it left the audience spellbound, their hearts beating in time with the rhythm of a cinematic symphony about to unfold.

Shantaram embarked on a cinematic odyssey unlike any other, a symphony of storytelling that transcended the boundaries of place and time. With each carefully crafted dialogue, each vivid description of unfolding scenarios, and the tender strains of supporting music caressing the air from his tiny harmonium, he beckoned the audience to join him on a two-hour joyride through realms of imagination and emotion.

In this mesmerising dance of narrative and melody, Shantaram wielded his solitary artistry like a maestro, orchestrating a journey that tugged at heartstrings and ignited a kaleidoscope of emotions within the enraptured spectators. Laughter bubbled forth in harmonious cadence with witty repartee, tears flowed freely in sync with poignant moments, and rounds of applause punctuated the air, a chorus of appreciation for the emotional rollercoaster they were privileged to witness.

As the intermission beckoned, a brief respite amidst the cinematic whirlwind, the audience lingered in a shared reverie, their spirits lifted by the magic unfurled before them. And in that delicate pause, my father, a paragon of compassion, extended a humble gesture of support, a simple cloth laid at Shantaram's feet, a vessel for the generosity of those moved by his artistry.

With heartfelt entreaties ringing in the air, the attendees, stirred by the spellbinding performance, came forward with whatever slivers of kindness they could muster. Though the initial offerings may have been modest, a mere thirty or forty rupees collected, the promise of further contributions lingered in the air like a whispered oath, a testament to the impact Shantaram had wrought upon their souls. In the symphony of shared emotion and communal support, the fabric of human connection was woven anew, binding hearts in a tapestry of generosity and shared appreciation.

With the sun dipping below the horizon, a silent procession began as early as seven in the evening, a parade of eager souls securing their spots with makeshift markers of old gunny bags, threadbare bed sheets, and tattered sarees strewn across the temple courtyard. The gathering swelled in size, doubling in numbers from the previous night, as whispers of Shantaram's mesmerising performance drew in the curious and captivated alike.

Amidst this sea of anticipation and communal fervour, a transformation unfolded—a symphony of generosity that mirrored the rising tide of enthusiasm. The offerings, no longer mere coins jingling in pockets, evolved into a profusion of abundance: grains, rice, and essential commodities, each symbolising a heartfelt tribute to the artistry that had touched their souls.

In this journey of communal unity, every contribution, whether tangible or intangible, echoed with a resonance of shared appreciation and unwavering support. The air buzzed with a palpable sense of communal spirit, as the humble offerings laid at Shantaram's feet served as a testament to the profound impact of his storytelling prowess, binding hearts in a harmony of generosity and shared delight.

The passage of the next seven days ushered in a transformative chapter in my young life, as the radiance of storytelling illuminated the precincts of Mahadev Temple's courtyard, courtesy of Shantaram's mesmerising one-man show. What commenced as a humble gathering on the first day blossomed into a magnificent spectacle by the seventh, drawing forth a throng of a thousand eager souls, each thirsting for the magic that only cinema could weave.

In the shadow of dusk and the incense-laden air, Shantaram's voice unfurled like a wide canvas of dreams, casting a spell upon the assembled villagers who gathered with bated breath. With each tale he spun, the air crackled with anticipation, hearts beating in unison to the rhythm of silver screen adventures about to unfold.

As the echoes of his narration reverberated through the temple courtyard, a symphony of emotions engulfed the audience. Their eyes, once fixed upon the mundane, now sparkled with the reflection of celluloid dreams conjured by Shantaram's fervent recitals. With a voice that danced between passion and poise, he breathed life into characters long confined to the realms of film reels, embodying each word with a fervour that transcended mere storytelling.

Three films garnered encore after encore by popular acclaim, their narratives painting vivid landscapes upon the canvas of the listeners' minds. Dialogues dripped like honey, melodies swirled like silk, and actions unfolded with a grace that defied the limits of a solitary performer. Shantaram wove a tapestry of visual splendour through the threads of his voice, bringing to life a spectacle that ignited the imagination and transported hearts to realms unknown.

In that sacred space where stories met souls, where the mundane mingled with the miraculous, Shantaram's one-man show transcended mere entertainment to become a transcendent experience. Each night beneath the starlit canopy, amidst the whispers of the wind and the rapt gazes of the enraptured audience, cinema found a new avatar in the form of a solitary storyteller, and I, a witness to this symphony of sight and sound, found myself forever changed by the magic that unfurled before me.

One profound insight I gleaned from a particular experience was the realisation that cinema transcends mere storytelling; it involves intricately manipulating audience emotions and effectively conveying a narrative. I discovered that the strength of a story lies not solely in its greatness, but in the skilful articulation, attention to detail, and the ability to resonate with the pulse of the audience. This valuable lesson became etched in my consciousness, serving as a guiding light in shaping my journey as a filmmaker.

Shantaram's magnetic performances did not just captivate hearts; they also garnered a tangible token of appreciation. The jingling of coins and rustling of notes filled his bag, a testament to the villagers' deep admiration for his craft. The weight of over six hundred and seventy-five rupees willingly bestowed upon him, a princely sum in the year 1970, spoke volumes of the impact Shantaram had woven into the fabric of their souls.

Yet, when Shantaram, with humility in his eyes, offered to cover his incurred expenses, my father's kindness shone through. With a dignified refusal, my father declined his offer, going a step further by adding twenty-five rupees to the pot to ensure a round figure. In this exchange of generosity and gratitude, a silent understanding blossomed—one that transcended mere monetary value and delved deeper into the realm of human connection and mutual respect.

A liking for storytelling blossomed within me. Meanwhile, my favourite pastime was recounting films to my peers with the gusto of a one-man show. I meticulously recreated the cinematic experience, enrapturing my friends with my renditions. Little did I know this early foray into storytelling would lay the groundwork for my future understanding of filmmaking.

During this period, travelling theatre troupes from Mumbai graced the Goan landscape, erecting makeshift theatres in paddy fields post-harvest. Our familial connections with professional actors afforded me the privilege of hosting these luminaries in our home. I eagerly accompanied them to their nightly performances, immersing myself in the intricacies of stagecraft—from set assembly to makeup application.

I have witnessed the assembly and dismantling of a revolving stage for a play, "Toh Me Navech". This magnificent innovation of that time was an experience in itself.

Seated outside the proscenium arch on the stage or nestled within the orchestra pit, I absorbed the nuances of performance, quizzing the actors on their craft with youthful curiosity. Their generosity in sharing their insights left an indelible mark on my understanding of the art form, paving the way for my own aspirations within the realm of theatre, ultimately leading to cinematic fantasy.

In my formative years, I had the extraordinary privilege of engaging with luminary figures of the theatre world. Shambhu Mitra, Kamlakar Sontakke, Jaidev Hattangady, Girish Karnad, Badal Sorkar, Vijaya Mehta, Satyadev Dubey, Kashinath Ghanekar, Satish Dubhashi, Damu Kenkre, and numerous others known and unknown interacted with me, impressed by my quest for the art form. These encounters proved so valuable as they imparted to me the intricate nuances of theatrical craftsmanship.

From discussions on the essence of character portrayal to the significance of plot development, from the nuances of diction to the complexities of inter-character relationships, these luminaries delved deep into the art of theatre. They elucidated the subtleties of situational dynamics, the importance of vocal modulation, the art of stage movement, and the manipulation of space and time to create immersive theatrical experiences.

Moreover, they shed light on the significance of language and textual analysis, the use of symbols and metaphors to convey deeper meaning, and the creation of mood and atmosphere to evoke emotional resonance. They expounded on the concept of audience engagement, the cultivation of dramatic tension, and the strategic utilisation of music to enhance the overall impact of a performance.

Through these interactions, I gained a profound appreciation for the multifaceted nature of theatre and acquired a wealth of knowledge that later enriched my own artistic endeavours within the realm of theatre and cinema.

When your mind becomes a repository of knowledge at such a tender age, it's easy to succumb to the illusion that you've already arrived at your destination. The sheer volume of insights and wisdom acquired from interactions with stalwarts of the craft can create a sense of premature accomplishment.

The icing on the cake came when I joined the renowned amateur theatre group of Goa, 'Kala Shuklendu,' in the year 1975 after my higher secondary school. From a small town of Curchorem, we moved to the capital city of Goa, Panjim. Kala Shuklendu was the epitome of creativity, known for their unconventional and experimental plays that pushed the boundaries of traditional theatre. From the moment I stepped foot into their midst, I felt a sense of belonging among this smart, young breed of modern theatre enthusiasts.

In a remarkable stroke of fate, my talent was recognised from the very first day. With my aura of confidence and passion, I quickly secured my place within the group. It was a whirlwind journey, filled with late-night rehearsals, intense workshops, and the thrill of bringing innovative ideas to life on stage.

In a stroke of serendipity, my debut performance garnered me the prestigious titles of Best Actor and Best Director at the state awards. It was a validation of my dedication and hard work, a moment of triumph that set the stage for what was to come.

As the days turned into weeks and the weeks into months, I emerged as an aspiring and respected figure in the world of theatre. Art lovers looked to me with great expectations, eager to witness the next groundbreaking production or awe-inspiring performance.

With each role I tackled and each production I directed, I embraced the opportunity to push the boundaries of my craft further. Every standing ovation and rave review fuelled my ambition, driving me to reach new heights of excellence in the world of theatre.

And as I stood on stage, bathed in the spotlight's glow, I knew I had found my calling. For in the world of theatre, where imagination knows no bounds and creativity reigns supreme, I had found my true passion and goal of life.

Life was unfolding before me like a well-scripted play, with each scene carefully crafted to shape my destiny. However, amidst the applause and accolades, loomed a shadow of disapproval cast by my strict father. He held firm to the belief that my priority should be completing my formal education before indulging in such extracurricular activities.

His disapproval manifested in tangible ways, such as cutting off my pocket money. Yet, he was not cruel in his actions, understanding that a headstrong youth like me would still require some financial support to navigate the challenges of life. Thus, he presented me with an alternative: a job at the newly opened milk centre.

The task was simple yet humbling—delivering milk bottles in the early hours of the morning, from 6:30 to 8:30, and ensuring the timely collection and transfer of cash to the dairy office. In return, I received a modest sum of seventy-five rupees per month, a meagre amount by today's standards but more than sufficient to sustain me in the year 1978.

This new responsibility added another layer of complexity to my already bustling life. Suddenly, I found myself thrust into the realm of self-sufficiency, no longer reliant on my parents' support to pursue my passions. My father, perhaps hoping to instil a sense of discipline and work ethic in me, had unwittingly ignited a fire of independence within me.

Yet, as I embraced this newfound autonomy, my arrogance began to swell. Each success in the theatre world further fuelled my confidence, blinding me to the lessons of humility and hard work that lay before me. I won several awards in local competitions for Acting, Direction, Music, Set design, and even Lighting design. And, as fate would have it, new developments soon entered the stage of my life, each one poised to shape the course of my journey in ways I could never have imagined.

The memory of that fateful day in January 1977 is etched into my mind like a scene from a vivid dream. I had just completed my second year in college and embarked on the journey of higher education in mechanical engineering, much to my father's insistence that I become a doctor. In those days, career options were limited to just three prestigious streams:

Doctor, Lawyer, and Engineer, with all other paths deemed of lesser importance.

It was in the midst of this tumultuous time that I encountered Baba Naik, a well-known local business personality, on the bustling streets of our town. He recognised me as a talented theatre enthusiast and beckoned me into a nearby restaurant for a cup of coffee.

Baba Naik was a prominent figure in the Indian film industry, revered for his role as a local production support supplier. He served as a liaison for Bollywood shooting units, coordinating their activities with precision and expertise. As actors, we were often hired as extras or crowd members for these shoots, our pockets lined with wages that, while modest, fuelled our passion for the craft.

Over coffee, Baba Naik wasted no time in getting to the heart of the matter. "Look, son," he began,

"I know you are very talented, and I know very well you want to be an actor. But having passion is just not enough. To be in the trade, you will have to be in the trade and establish yourself with strong foundations."

"Come to the point, Baba." My expected arrogant answer.

"One Hollywood unit is coming for a shoot in Goa, and I need hard-working, smart..."

"Actors!" My impatient reaction.

"No. Production Assistants," Baba said with a strong, sharp look at me, anticipating my next reaction.

I had no clue what a 'Production Assistant' was.

"You will be assisting me and helping me in my work." - Baba.

"Of course, you will be paid well... Ten rupees per day."

He must have seen a strong glitter in my eyes. So, he added further, "Paid every day after day's work."

Baba Naik's words echoed in my mind, cutting through the haze of excitement and uncertainty that clouded my thoughts.

Imagine my state of mind at the age of twenty when someone is ready to pay this much amount of money. I did not even blink and said, "Yes, I'm in."

There is a saying that in order to gain something, one must be willing to lose something in return. At that particular moment, this concept hadn't quite registered with me—I had never stopped to consider what I might have to loose. The glamorous world of Hollywood and filmmaking beckoned, presenting itself as a golden opportunity that I simply couldn't afford to miss. So, without fully *realising* the consequences, I enthusiastically accepted the offer, committing nearly thirty crucial days to the project, right when my college exams loomed ahead. Ignoring the implications of further complexities.

I deceived my father and threw myself wholeheartedly into the demanding schedule of the shoot of 'Sea Wolves'.

The roster of talent involved was impressive—Gregory Peck, Roger Moore, and David Niven, along with Indian actors like Mohan Agashe, Keith Stevenson, and Mark Zuber were slated to be part of the production. The eminent production designer Syd Chain arrived early, setting the tone for a flurry of activity as other key personnel also streamed in. Amidst the hustle and bustle, Mario Cabral e Sa took charge as the unit manager in Goa, while Mohamed Shafi assumed the role of Production Manager for the Indian leg of the shoot. Baba Naik was our only single-point contact.

Being a relatively small player in this grand operation, I found myself in awe of the proceedings—lurking in the background, absorbing insights from the strategic conversations of seasoned professionals. The Hotel Fidalgo in Panjim, Goa, graciously accommodated the expanding crew by offering additional rooms. Modified buses served as makeshift vanity and wardrobe vans, underscoring the grandeur of the production.

Words like vanity, gaffer, grips, wrangler, storyboard, rigger, HMI, flags, FPS, dolly, baby, day-for-night, call sheet, best boy, body double, barn doors (popularly called bandoors), apple box, atmosphere, and wrap I heard for the first time. There was one young white man working in the unit. I vaguely remember his name; someone called him Andrew. I had no clue what his position was in the unit. Whenever asked, he said, "I am a PA in this unit." Until the end of the shoot, I thought it was 'personnel assistant'. Much later, I came to know he was a production assistant.

My position in the hierarchy was humble—perhaps the fourth or fifth, if not further down the ladder of production assistants. Bestowed with the title "Motorcycle Wrangler," I was tasked with shuttle responsibilities on a meagre bike. Our primary duty involved prep work at advance locations and post-shoot clean-ups, leaving us with little exposure to the actual filming process. Our only glimpses of the actors were fleeting encounters in the hotel lobby, where we shamelessly seized any opportunity to catch a glimpse of the glamorous world unfolding before us.

This encounter with a major film production significantly redirected my attention from the realm of theatre to the glamorous world of celluloid.

Interacting with actors and technicians who descended upon Goa for film shoots, I found myself captivated by their stories and experiences. Each one of them emphasised that to truly make a mark in the film industry, one needed to venture to Bombay, the epicentre of Indian cinema.

Moreover, certain budding actors, who themselves were on the brink of stardom, took notice of my theatre background and praised my abilities extensively. Their words of encouragement echoed with conviction as they urged me to consider Mumbai as the building ground for talents like mine. The allure of Mumbai's film industry grew stronger with each endorsement, painting a picture of endless opportunities and the potential for growth and recognition.

This feeling of having "arrived" prematurely is akin to standing at the foot of a mountain, armed with a map of its summit, and believing you've already scaled its heights. Yet, in reality, the journey has only just begun.

While early exposure to profound knowledge is undeniably enriching, *it is* essential to *recognise* that true mastery is a lifelong pursuit. Each new piece of information is but a stepping stone on the path to deeper understanding and mastery of one's craft. So, rather than resting on the laurels of early knowledge, *it is* crucial to remain humble, curious, and committed to continuous growth and learning; only then can one truly ascend to the summit of their aspirations.

Having somehow managed to scrape through my engineering education with dismal passing marks, I harboured no illusions about securing a decent job with such a lacklustre academic record. Determined to pursue my dream in Mumbai, I found myself at odds with my parents, especially during a particularly heated argument where I expressed my desire to make the move.

In the midst of the intense disagreement, my father eventually relented, unable to dissuade me from my chosen path. While my mother attempted to mediate between my father and me, my stubborn resolve remained unyielding, deaf to the well-intentioned advice that surrounded me.

Finally, my father laid down the ultimatum: I could indeed go to Mumbai under one strict condition. I was to fend for myself entirely—without the support of any relatives or a single penny from my parents, barring a small sum for initial expenses. If I could sustain myself, I could stay; if not, I was to return, where my father promised to secure me a respectable job.

Agreeing to these terms, I affirmed that I would not rely on any familial connections and resolved to carve out my future in Mumbai. Despite my expectations of my father's recognition of my confidence, his seasoned perspective saw through my bravado, silently lamenting, "God help this overconfident son of mine."

❖

2

AMBITIOUS MISTAKES

Ambitions can sometimes lead us down a path where mistakes are inevitable. Our fervent desire to achieve our dreams and reach our goals can cloud our judgment, causing us to make errors along the way. While ambition is a powerful driving force that propels us forward, it can also blind us to potential pitfalls and challenges that may lie ahead. It's important to channel our ambitions wisely, remaining open to learning from our mistakes and using them as stepping stones toward growth and success. Each misstep can offer valuable lessons that ultimately shape us into wiser, more resilient individuals on the journey towards realising our ambitions.

Ambitions, while fuelling our drive for success, can sometimes lead us into traps if we're not careful. One common trap is becoming too narrowly focused on a single goal, neglecting other important aspects of our lives such as relationships, health, or personal well-being. This tunnel vision can blind us to potential risks and cause us to overlook warning signs along the way.

Another trap is setting unrealistic expectations for ourselves, leading to feelings of inadequacy or failure if we do not meet these lofty goals. This can create undue pressure and stress, ultimately hampering our ability to perform at our best.

Furthermore, the relentless pursuit of ambitions can sometimes tempt us to compromise our values or integrity in the pursuit of success. It's crucial to stay true to ourselves and our principles, even in the face of external pressures or temptations.

Ultimately, being mindful of the potential traps that ambitions can set for us is key to navigating our path to success with grace and resilience. Balancing our drive for achievement with self-awareness, flexibility, and a holistic view of success can help us avoid these pitfalls and stay on course towards our goals.

Arriving in the bustling city of Mumbai, all alone, in 1980, with just a small suitcase filled with clothes and a trove of certificates highlighting my excellence in theatre, I found myself at a crossroads.

Mumbai held a familiar charm for me, a city that welcomed my presence every summer vacation alongside my mother. Our abode during these enchanting visits was the luxurious five-thousand-square-foot flat positioned on the pinnacle, the fifth floor, of my maternal grandmother's opulent building. Each year, my heart yearned for that one month of resplendent escapade. The vibrancy of the film industry reached its zenith during those delightful summers. And oh, the tales I would carry to Goa, narrating stories of newly unveiled films, for in those times, movies took over three months to grace the screens of Goa.

Witnessing the grandeur of a 70 mm spectacle like 'Sholay' at the illustrious Minerva Cinema Hall left an indelible imprint on my memory. I can vividly recall the significant date - the film's grand debut on the 15th of August in bustling Mumbai. How serendipitous it was that I embarked on my Mumbai sojourn with my mother during the Diwali vacation in October, a time marked by a festive aura permeating the air, evoking a sense of magic and wonder.

Near my granny's house, an array of iconic cinema halls such as Minerva, Apsara, Dreamland, Shalimar, Naaz, Roxy, Alankar, Majestic, Imperial, and Central Cinema stood in close proximity. It was a simple stroll for me to reach these theatres and indulge in watching films. Interestingly, I had a penchant for experiencing movies in solitude; unlike many, I never opted to watch a film accompanied by friends or in a group.

A notable learning experience transpired during my one-month theatre workshop in Mumbai in 1978. Having won the Best Actor and Best Director awards in the Maharashtra state drama competition, I was chosen from Goa to participate in this workshop, fully sponsored by the government. Our daily schedule involved watching a movie or theatre play after our workshop sessions. Each morning, we engaged in discussions critiquing the previous night's viewing and analysing our preferences and criticisms. One day, I expressed my disapproval of a play I had watched. In response, Damu Kenkre, a renowned theatre director and set designer, delivered a strong rebuke. He challenged my simplistic opinion, reminding me of the immense effort involved in the production process. With cutting words, he said, "You are not Stanislavsky," emphasising the importance of understanding and respecting the hard work behind each artistic endeavour. This unforgettable moment served as a wake-up call, instilling in me a lasting reverence for art and a commitment to thoughtful critique based on understanding and justification.

As an exercise, I started watching movies on videotape in 1982 and began writing down each scene. This helped me understand how a screenplay is constructed.

Back again, on my journey to Mumbai, I had a disagreement with my parents and travelled to Mumbai alone.

Disembarking from the bus that had carried me from Goa, I arrived in Dhobi Talao, where I perched on a bus stop bench, observing the hurried pace of life unfolding around me. It felt as if I was a passive spectator in a whirlwind of activity, unsure of my place in this dynamic urban landscape.

Between 1962 and 1980, the city underwent massive transformations. The sights of my early childhood had vanished - trams, large taxis, bullock carts, and horse carriages were missing. They were my beautiful memories of the truly magnificent Mumbai. Tall modern structures obscured the few remaining vestiges of the past. Standing prominently amidst these changes was the Metro Theatre, a steadfast reminder of bygone days, right before my eyes.

My father's unwavering directive reverberated in my mind: "You will not seek help from any relative."

Despite his words ringing persistently in my ears, a sense of desolation washed over me. I grappled with a wave of emotions—frustration, self-doubt, and regret gnawing at me for my impulsive decisions and my brusque interactions with my parents. In that moment of vulnerability, the idea of boarding the next bus back to Goa beckoned, a tempting escape from the uncertainties that loomed ahead.

Yet, amidst this turmoil, a whisper of resolve stirred within me, urging me to rise to the challenge—to fight against the odds and give this new chapter a chance. Summoning the words of a famous movie dialogue, I muttered to myself, "Jiska koi nahi hota, uska Bhagwan hota hai" (He who has no one, has God by his side).

This mantra of resilience and faith in the face of adversity provided a flicker of hope in the midst of my uncertainty, nudging me to persevere and dare to carve out my own path in the unfamiliar expanse of Mumbai.

I looked around and in the distance, saw my uncle (my dad's elder brother) walking towards the bus stop where I was sitting. Initially, he was shocked to see me sitting alone at the bus stop. I told him that I had just arrived to pursue my career.

"Where have you put up?" - My uncle
"Not decided anything yet." - me.

Honesty is indeed a valuable trait, fostering trust and integrity in our interactions with others. Being truthful not only builds stronger relationships but also cultivates a sense of authenticity and accountability within ourselves. While it may be tempting to deceive or withhold the truth in certain situations, practising honesty ultimately leads to transparency and fosters genuine connections with those around us. Remember, being honest not only benefits others but also contributes to our own personal growth and self-respect.

I explained openly to him. My uncle was always known as the most kind-hearted person in the entire family. He offered me to stay in our ancestral house. He also promised that he would not tell or let my short-tempered father know that I was staying with him. "Stay for a few days and when you feel you can manage, move on."

I deceived my father and took shelter in my uncle's house. I convinced my flickering mind that "Anyway, it's my ancestral property, so there's no harm in taking temporary shelter."

Deceiving someone for the perceived sake of their betterment is a complex ethical dilemma. While the intention behind such deception may be well-meaning, it's important to consider the potential consequences of withholding the truth. In the short term, the person being deceived might not experience immediate harm or distress if they remain unaware of certain information. However, in the long run, the discovery of this deception could lead to a significant breach of trust and damage the relationship.

This impulsive decision was one big mistake of mine. At that moment, I never felt like I was committing a mistake because – *Setting goals in life is essential for personal growth.* Goals provide direction, focus, and a sense of purpose, guiding us towards our aspirations and dreams. They help us prioritise our time and energy, create a roadmap for success, and challenge us to push our boundaries and achieve our full potential.

I decided to give my dream a chance in Mumbai for a short period. If, after this trial period, I am unable to make headway, I would then consider returning to Goa. This symbolised a pivotal moment of commitment and determination as I embarked on this new chapter in pursuit of my aspirations.

I moved in with my uncle, a decision that was met with resistance from my aunt. Her reluctance stemmed from a complex backstory that coloured her perception of my presence in their home. She harboured suspicions, believing that my stay was motivated by ulterior motives. Specifically, she doubted that my father had orchestrated this move as part of a larger scheme to stake a claim on the family's ancestral property.

Indeed, fear and doubt have the potential to hinder relationships in various ways. When fear or doubt creeps into a relationship, it can erode trust, create distance, and breed uncertainty among individuals. Communication may become strained as doubts linger unaddressed, leading to misunderstandings and misinterpretations.

On my part, I made a conscious effort not to disrupt their daily routine. I intended to utilise their home solely as a place to stay, rather than as a base for my activities or boarding.

For a newcomer, entering the film industry may seem like a relatively straightforward task, driven by passion and ambition. However, the true challenge lies in sustaining a career amidst the competitive and ever-evolving landscape of the entertainment world. While making an initial mark through opportunities or projects may be achievable with dedication and perseverance, maintaining relevance and longevity in the industry demands ongoing dedication, resilience, and adaptability. It requires navigating through intense competition, unpredictable market trends, and the constant demand for innovation and creativity. Success in the film industry is not just about making a debut; it's about constantly evolving, honing one's craft, building enduring relationships, and staying committed to the journey despite the inevitable setbacks and uncertainties that come with the territory. For all, the most important factor is financial stability.

It was precisely due to this realisation that I chose to accept the first job offer that came my way as a draftsman in an architectural firm. Given my proficiency in drafting, which was honed during my years at engineering college, I was offered a modest monthly stipend of four hundred rupees. While this compensation may not have been extravagant, it allowed me to make ends meet and sustain myself during that period.

My routine was set. From 9.00 am to 6.00 pm in the architect's office, and after that, I would try to meet all those stalwarts who had invited me with very high hopes.

In my personal experience, I have encountered individuals who excel at painting grand illusions of support and promises, showering me with lofty hopes and assurances. However, when the time comes for tangible assistance or genuine help, their *demeanour* swiftly shifts, and they conveniently turned a blind eye to my needs. This stark contrast between the appearance of unwavering support and the reality of their actions has been a poignant lesson in discerning genuine allies from those who merely offer empty promises. It has underscored the importance of relying on those who demonstrate consistent actions and genuine care rather than being swayed by superficial displays of support that ultimately prove to be illusory.

I will not mention anyone's name who actually shattered my hopes with their strange behaviour. Some were very good, some were bad. The distinction between good and bad people is often subjective and complex, as an individual's actions and intentions can vary widely based on circumstances, perspectives, and personal values. In general terms, society often categorises individuals as 'good' if they display qualities such as kindness, empathy, honesty, and integrity, while 'bad' people may exhibit behaviours like selfishness or dishonesty. However, it's important to recognise that people are not inherently good or bad but rather a nuanced combination of virtues and flaws. Human beings are capable of growth, change, and redemption, making it essential to consider the context and motivations behind their actions.

Most of them told me that it is very difficult to establish a foothold in Mumbai. Some even refused to acknowledge me. This was like a big jolt. Were all those who instilled big dreams in my mind just engaging in empty rhetoric?

"Where have we met? In Goa? Maybe, but I am tied up for the next six months. Meet me after six months; we will see what we can do." These were the words of an eminent actor and director of that time who once said, "Come to Mumbai. I have a theatre group and production house. I can surely help you in Mumbai."

For me, even sustaining for six days was difficult. My job was helping me a little bit, but it was not enough. The lifestyle in Mumbai was expensive even then.

On the other hand, the situation at my Aunt's place was also not promising

"If you reach home by 8.00 pm, you will get dinner; otherwise, you will need to take care of yourself."

My aunt told me upfront as I always arrived around 10.00 pm. The typical so-called struggle was allowed only for three hours, which was too little. I decided to skip dinner. Wada Pao was there for survival. Yet, I was meeting people with high hopes.

"I dimly remember seeing your play."

"You came to see my play 'Baki Eitihas' and congratulated me for a stunning performance. In fact, you said I was much superior to professional actors who staged the play in Mumbai."

"Really! Did I say that? Maybe."

This was my interaction with another very famous director, whom I met when I was selected for a one-month special training in theatre by the Maharashtra government in 1978.

Our rendezvous at the Rabindra Natya Mandir for this transformative month was nothing short of magical and entrancing. Amidst the creative ambience of this sanctuary for performing arts, I forged valuable and enduring friendships, bonding with fellow enthusiasts who shared in this collective immersion into the world of theatre and creativity. The shared experiences, learnings, and camaraderie woven during this period left an indelible mark on my soul, enriching my artistic sensibilities and fostering a sense of belonging within this vibrant artistic community.

Upon my return in 1980, the ostensible glamour of big stars and celebrities inadvertently obscured my practical sensibilities, casting a shadow over my innate instincts. The cutting remarks and piercing words emanating from these individuals continued to echo relentlessly, etching deep imprints on my psyche even in my later years. Confronted with such unwarranted negativity, the only recourse left to me was to meticulously excise their names from the corridors of my memory, relinquishing their hold on my thoughts and reclaiming my inner peace.

Day by day, my hopes and dreams were shattering into pieces. Yet, I was trying to collect all the shattered pieces and join them in anticipation.

It's clear that I was facing a tough time trying to piece together the fragments of my hopes and dreams. The process of rebuilding after setbacks can be both challenging and rewarding. By persisting in my efforts to gather the shattered pieces and mend them, I was demonstrating resilience and strength in the face of adversity. Each step I took towards reassembling my aspirations brought me closer to a stronger, more resilient sense of myself and purpose. I kept moving forward, and I know that setbacks are often stepping stones towards growth and eventual success.

Destiny was testing my patience every day. Another strict rule was implemented by my aunt. They started locking the main door and refused to give me the latch keys. I rang the bell maybe once or twice, but she made a nasty remark. It was truly humiliating.

"Either you come home by nine pm or sleep on the terrace. Don't disturb our sleep as we have to get up early. For a few days, I slept on the water tank on the terrace without any mattress, under the sky, watching the stars and daydreaming at night. Entry into the house was only in the morning with the milkman."

The restricted entry conditions imposed on me further compounded the sense of isolation and discomfort that I was experiencing. These trying situations likely tested my patience and resilience, highlighting the importance of finding inner strength and seeking support during tough times. Reaching out for help and exploring alternatives can offer solace and assistance in navigating such challenging circumstances.

In such moments of doubt and uncertainty, it's important to remember that setbacks are a natural part of any journey towards success. Each shattered piece represents an opportunity for growth, learning, and eventual progress. By remaining determined and resilient in the face of adversity, you demonstrate your strength and commitment to your goals. While the road may seem daunting and lonely at times, know that perseverance and belief in yourself can ultimately help you to navigate the challenges and uncertainties.

Setbacks do not define your potential for success; *instead*, they provide valuable lessons and experiences that can shape your path forward. Stay resilient, stay hopeful, and keep working towards rebuilding your dreams, piece by piece. *What* you need at this juncture is the *interaction* with the right person.

The first person of integrity I encountered amidst the bustling expanse of Mumbai was a Parsi man, Sheriyar Tirandaz, the proprietor of Jai Bharat Bar and Restaurant. Situated conveniently opposite my architect's office, this humble establishment provided me with a unique opportunity. Sheriyar graciously extended a three-hour job to manage his cash counter at the bar, offering me meals at his restaurant in return for my service.

Seeking guidance and advice from the right people can indeed make a significant difference in our lives. Surrounding ourselves with individuals who offer support, wisdom, and constructive feedback can help us navigate challenges, make informed decisions, and grow personally and professionally. The insights and perspectives shared by the right mentors, friends, or advisors can provide valuable clarity, inspiration, and direction on our journey towards success and fulfilment. By cultivating strong relationships with those who have our best interests at heart and who offer sound advice, we enhance our ability to overcome obstacles, seize opportunities, and ultimately achieve our goals.

Realising and sharing our mistakes with the right person is a crucial part of personal growth and self-improvement.

Finding the right person who offers support and understanding can be a significant turning point in challenging times.

It was like reaching a breaking point after a heated argument with my aunt, leading me to make the decision to leave her house and walk out with my few belongings.

The uncertainty of the situation and the impending night ahead weighed heavily on my mind throughout the day. The passing of time felt accelerated, each moment filled with contemplation and anticipation of what the evening would bring after work. It's during such moments of upheaval and transition that the support and guidance of the right people can offer comfort and direction, helping navigate through uncertainties and challenges.

Leaving my possessions at the office, I made my way to Jai Bharat Bar and Restaurant with the intention of discussing my predicament with Sheriyar. However, despite my best efforts, I found myself unable to muster the courage to open up to him. True to the nature of dear friends who intuitively grasp your unspoken troubles, Sheriyar sensed that all was not well. Without any words exchanged, he kindly offered me a complimentary drink, a gesture of understanding and support during a tough time.

Shadows dancing around me. The weight of my impulsive decisions bore down on me as I sought refuge in a few drinks, drowning my sorrows as the memories of better days played out in my mind like a bittersweet symphony.

As the nearby grocery shop shuttered its windows for the night, casting a final glimpse of light on the darkened street, I eyed a wooden flap - a potential makeshift bed. The chatter of a group of men already occupying the spot added to the tension, forcing me to bide my time. Lost in my thoughts, the abrupt voice of Sheriyar shattered my reverie like breaking glass.

"Don't feel like going home? I mean your aunt's place."

"I will; my terrace is waiting for me, and to sleep on the terrace I don't have any restrictions of time."

Longing for one more round of beer to numb the ache within, I reached for my wallet only to find emptiness staring back at me. With a heavy heart, I stepped out into the night. The group on the wooden plank continued their animated conversation, their voices echoing through the dimly lit alleys.

Setting off on foot, the flashing yellow light of a nearby signal beckoned, offering a fleeting glimmer of hope amidst the darkness. The absence of the dreaded red light brought a flicker of relief, a small spark of tranquillity in the midst of my tumultuous journey.

As I wandered aimlessly, the inviting call of a nearby garden beckoned me nearer. The gentle whisper of the trees seemed to say, "Come, rest upon these benches generously gifted by kind souls. Find solace in this tranquil sanctuary."

Taking a seat on the very first bench I encountered, I was enveloped by the comforting shadows cast by the sprawling banyan tree above me. The soft moonlight filtered through its branches, casting an ethereal glow. Nearby, wisps of smoke from a smouldering fire danced in the air, painting the scene with delicate streaks of light. What had once been a backdrop for a film shoot, now unfolded before me in all its authentic splendour.

Feeling a surge of poetry stirring within me, words began to form in my mind:

"We enter this world from the depths of a dark womb,
Unfamiliar with the harsh light beyond.
Yet, we seek out brightness upon our arrival,
For the world's darkness slowly reveals itself.
After each stumble, the allure of the shadows beckons,
Yet a glimmer of hope stands at the threshold,
Amidst the ceaseless carousel of life's twists and turns,
We yearn to break free from this cycle's grip,
Though we find ourselves spinning round and round,
Ensnared by the gravitational pull of the darkness that surrounds.

I experienced a fleeting sense of elation as my creative thoughts flowed freely. However, this moment of happiness was short-lived. A police constable approached me, disrupting my reverie as he nudged me with his cane.

"Hello! Get up. This is not the place for sleeping at this hour. How did you come in here?" he demanded sternly.

"Apologies, sir... The gate was open, so I..." I began before being abruptly cut off.

"Move along immediately," he commanded.

Reluctantly, I rose from the bench and stepped back into the stark reality of the night.

It was almost one hour past midnight. I decided to wait at the nearby bus stop until morning. As I was walking towards the bus stop, I realised that I was standing in front of the beautiful drama theatre Ravindra Natya Mandir.

I quickly moved into a flashback of 1978 when I stayed there as a student of theatre for one month. I was looking at the gate, which was partially open, and remembered the tragic scene of helping a dead drunk superstar of the Marathi stage. No one could believe at that time that he was the only superstar of the stage in that era. He was the one who always came to my house in my childhood days in Goa. My father and he were good friends. Later on, he became a big star but never forgot the friendship.

From him, at a young age, I gleaned a valuable lesson on the distinction between method acting and spontaneous acting. His ability to effortlessly embody characters on stage left me spellbound. Curious, I once mustered the courage to ask him, "How do you perform in such a mesmerising manner? Is there a specific technique you follow?" Amidst a successful theatre tour, he regarded me with surprise and admiration. It was unexpected for him to receive such a complex query from a seven or eight-year-old child hailing from a small village like Curshorem in Goa. After a brief pause, he shared a profound insight with me - "There is no technique for acting. Perform with technique, and your portrayal becomes mechanical. The audience will see you as an actor playing a role. However, if you can dive into the essence of the character's soul, they will embrace you as that character." This revelation initially seemed beyond my grasp, like a baffling mystery. Yet, as I delved into the world of theatre in later years, I came to realise the essence of spontaneous acting versus method acting, and how authenticity and immersion can transcend mere technique in captivating an audience.

The irony was palpable as we witnessed a superstar actor of such calibre struggling to rise from the ground before us. At that moment, confusion clouded my thoughts - was he genuinely inebriated, or was he portraying a drunken act with such conviction? Without hesitation, my colleagues from the theatre workshop and I came to his aid, lifting him up and ushering him inside.

Irony is a literary device that involves a discrepancy between what is expected and what actually occurs. It often serves to highlight contrasts, contradictions, or unexpected twists in a situation, leading to a sense of incongruity or *humour*. In real-life scenarios, irony can add depth and complexity to our understanding of events or experiences, revealing the nuances and contradictions inherent in human existence. *Recognising* irony can prompt us to reflect on the complexities of life and the unpredictability of outcomes, prompting us to consider alternative perspectives and embrace the unexpected in our journey.

As I attempted to rise from my position on the ground, I realised a strange numbness had overtaken me, a consequence, perhaps, of exhaustion and sleep deprivation.

"Sir! What are you doing here? I recognise you. You're Kashyap, right? I used to serve you tea daily when you were here for the workshop. Remember?" he exclaimed.

He was Shivaji, the watchman at the Ravindra Natya Mandir. The familiarity and warmth in his recognition filled me with delight and a profound sense of joy—knowing that in this unfamiliar city, someone recognised me as a theatre person.

Explaining my predicament of having lost my room keys and unable to find a locksmith at that late hour, I concocted the only explanation that came to mind, "I must have dropped them somewhere here."

With a reassuring smile, Shivaji invited me inside, suggesting I wait on the benches near the statue of Rabindranath Tagore in the foyer. He reminisced about the workshop where I had narrated the story of "Charulata," the tale of the lonely wife of a newspaper editor who finds solace in literature.

Acknowledging the memory briefly, I halted the conversation, my mind unable to delve into the past at that moment. Together, we walked inside, where I found solace on a wooden bench, slipping into a bow and arrow position, my hands outstretched towards Rabindranath Tagore's statue, perhaps in a silent homage to the recognition Charulata had brought me in the bustling city of Mumbai.

I woke to Shivaji's urgent whispers, coaxing me back to consciousness. Through bleary eyes, I checked the time—it was close to 6:00 am. Sensing

Shivaji's anxiety, I inquired about the situation, eager to understand the cause of his distress.

"My boss spotted you sleeping on the bench and instructed me to bring you to his cabin. He's a strict man, sir. Please, you must help me. If he discovers I allowed you inside, he'll surely dismiss me," Shivaji pleaded, his expression fraught with worry.

Assuring Shivaji that I would intervene, I rose, splashed cool water on my face in the washroom, and made my way towards the boss's cabin. Shivaji's beseeching gaze followed me as I approached the looming confrontation.

Upon knocking, a stern voice commanded me to enter. The boss, a man in his fifties with thinning hair and thick-rimmed glasses, scrutinised me intently as I stood before him. Invited to sit, I faced a direct question about my presence and the circumstances that led me to sleep within the premises, demanding a candid response.

Caught in a moment of truth, I hesitated briefly, realising the gravity of the scenario. Choosing not to reiterate the excuse of a lost key, I grappled with the importance of honesty and sincerity in navigating the impending conversation. As the situation unfolded, the values of integrity, authenticity, and transparency remained forefront in guiding my actions and shaping my interactions.

In a nutshell, I recounted my journey from Goa to Mumbai in pursuit of my ambitious dreams, detailing my experiences in the world of theatre, struggles with relatives, and moments of confrontation. In a moment of vulnerability, I bared it all to him.

Faced with the weight of my confessions, he extended a glass of water, which I eagerly downed in one go. Expressing understanding towards the challenges faced by young individuals venturing into Mumbai, he revealed a shared background of overcoming hardships.

"You seem to come from a decent family. I can understand how you young guys come to Mumbai and struggle. I have also come a hard way. I hope you know me?"

I acknowledged Dr Vishwas Mehendale, Director of Cultural Affairs at the Maharashtra government, whose signature adorned my certificates as a two-time silver medal awardee in state competitions.

"How much do you earn for a living? Those medals will not fetch anything for your day-to-day needs." - Dr Mehendale.

"Good enough to survive," I answered. Actually, my salary was just four hundred rupees, but I had no guts to admit it.

"We have some rooms in this premises, basically for outstation artists who come to Mumbai for a short period. I can allocate you one room for a period of one month. It will cost you three hundred rupees per month. If it's affordable, you can deposit the rent in advance and start staying here."

Belief in a higher power providing guidance and assistance to genuine individuals is a comforting and hopeful sentiment. Many find solace in the idea that acts of sincerity, kindness, and authenticity are recognised and supported by a divine force or by the universe itself. This faith in divine intervention in the lives of those who strive to be true to themselves and uphold values of honesty and integrity can offer a sense of reassurance and purpose in challenging times. Embracing the notion that goodness is rewarded and that benevolent forces are at play can provide comfort, strength, and motivation to navigate life's obstacles in the path of destiny.

The irony of destiny lies in the unexpected twists, turns, and contradictions that life presents us with. It is in those moments when what we anticipate or strive for contrasts sharply with what actually unfolds. Destiny, with its mysterious ways, often brings about outcomes that defy our expectations, challenging our beliefs and plans.

This irony can manifest in various forms: dreams shattered only to lead to new opportunities, paths diverging to reveal uncharted territories, or fortunes changing in the blink of an eye. The unpredictability of destiny underscores the intricate dance between fate and free will, highlighting the complexities of human existence. It invites us to appreciate the paradoxes, mysteries, and uncertainties that shape our journeys, reminding us that sometimes the most profound lessons are learned through the unexpected turns orchestrated by destiny.

For a span of nearly six months, my abode was the illustrious Ravindra Natya Mandir, diligently meeting my rent dues and adeptly balancing my finances to eke out a mere surplus of a hundred rupees. The progression from a modest income of four hundred rupees to a substantially improved four thousand over the course of four transformative years, from 1982 to 1985, marked a period of incremental growth and financial stability.

The winds of change beckoned, prompting my transition to diverse, yet economically viable rented accommodations. Embracing the vibrant world of amateur theatre, I became an integral part of revered theatrical groups such as 'Ya Mandali Sadar Karuya' and 'Maitra Mumbai'. Through the enactment of several plays, I encountered kindred spirits and forged friendships that transcended time. Among these cherished companions were Prakash Kamat, Ashok Gangavane, Samar Desai, Hemant Limaye, Dhanesh Jukar, Ravi Hirlekar, Pratibha, Bhagyashree, and a host of others, whose camaraderie and shared passion for the art form wove the fabric of unforgettable memories and enduring bonds.

In this profound period of transformation, my life took a drastic turn as I made pivotal decisions to align my path with my true aspirations. Driven by an unwavering commitment to my dreams, I veered away from architecture in 1985, recognising that it did not resonate with my innermost desires. Embracing a new chapter as a freelancer in the entertainment industry, albeit with financial constraints, I found solace in the fulfilment derived from pursuing my long-cherished goals. Concurrently, my fervour for theatre continued to thrive, with a blend of professional engagements and active involvement in amateur theatrical endeavours.

Through the serendipitous intertwining of fates, I found an unspoken harmony with Bhagyashree, a kindred spirit whose unwavering support and shared vision made her my true life companion. Our destinies intertwined as we embarked on a journey together, transcending all boundaries of time and adversity. Bhagyashree, the steadfast pillar of my existence, has been a beacon of unwavering strength through life's tumultuous seas, anchoring me in moments of despair and uplifting me through life's highs and lows. Her presence has been the guiding light that has steered me through the storms, preventing my life from descending into chaos and disarray.

The culmination of this transformative period was sealed with our union in marriage to Bhagyashree, the beloved daughter of Dr Vishwas Mehendale, in the year 1989. The very same Dr Vishwas Mehendale who uplifted me from the shadows of the footpath, weaving threads of decency and dignity into the fabric of my existence. This union heralded a new chapter infused with love and resilience. Unwavering partnership with Bhagyashree is like a bond that continues to weather the tests of time and fortify our souls against life's adversities.

❖

3

RIGHT PLACE, RIGHT TIME

Balancing the benefits and potential pitfalls of being in the right place at the right time involves a combination of mindfulness, readiness, and strategic action. While seizing opportune moments can yield significant advantages, it's essential to complement this with proactive efforts, preparedness, and a long-term vision to maintain sustainable growth and success.

Identifying the right place and the right time involves a combination of self-awareness, intuition, preparedness, and openness to opportunities.

This concept underscores the significance of readiness, awareness, and receptivity to seize advantageous moments as they present themselves. It emphasises the importance of being prepared, open-minded, and proactive in recognising and making the most of favourable circumstances. While chance plays a role in these occurrences, being attuned to possibilities and having the courage to act can help us make the most of fortuitous situations that come our way.

My resourcefulness started shining through as I established Rabindra Natya Mandir as both my dwelling and networking hub, immersing myself in a vibrant cultural environment. Navigating the constraints of a meagre budget of a hundred rupees, I not only upheld my rent obligations but also deftly managed other expenses. My persistence in fostering connections with professional producers, who frequented the premises for rehearsals, underscored my dedication and adaptability in navigating the industry landscape.

Introducing fellow artists to Jai Bharat Restaurant and Bar for leisurely post-rehearsal gatherings spoke about my generosity and social acumen. As the establishment welcomed guests past midnight, it offered a welcoming respite for hardworking professionals seeking relaxation and camaraderie after late-night performances.

My ability to cultivate relationships has cultivated a supportive network, further facilitating moments of bonding amidst challenging circumstances. This has showcased my resilience and proactive spirit. These endeavours have not only deepened my cultural immersion but also paved the way for enduring connections and opportunities within the industry.

One fateful day, as my roommate Prasad and I leisurely strolled down the street opposite Rabindra Natya Mandir, the universe seemed to align in perfect harmony. Prasad, much like myself, had ventured from Goa to Mumbai in pursuit of a career as a cinematographer, working diligently as an assistant to the esteemed cinematographer of that era, K Vaikunth. He was also showcasing his musical talents as a guitarist. Together, we had spent countless late nights immersed in heartfelt jam sessions, using music to cleanse our shared sorrows. A spontaneous decision led us to step into the theatre, and as fate would have it, we found ourselves amid a drama rehearsal. Welcomed by familiar faces, we were invited inside to witness the theatrical magic in progress. The director, intrigued by the guitar in my hands, inquired about my musical abilities. Introducing Prasad, we were unexpectedly offered roles in the play, to which we eagerly and unequivocally agreed.

Little did we know that this serendipitous moment would unleash a series of events that would go down in history on the Marathi stage. The play proved to be a turning point for many involved - transforming aspiring theatre enthusiasts into shining stars who would go on to carve their names in the annals of the industry. Laxmikant Berde, Prashant Damle, Vijay Kenkre, Chetan Dalvi, Vijay Kadam, and Vijay Chavan. All of them made it very big and became very successful with their hard work. In that moment, it became abundantly clear - sometimes, being in the right place at the right time can set the stage for remarkable destinies to unfold.

It was a momentous breakthrough when I took my first step onto the professional stage as an actor, selected to play a supporting role in the path-breaking Marathi play "Tour Tour" in the year 1982. While the main star commanded a fee of 350 rupees per show, my debut as a supporting actor earned me a humble 50 rupees per performance. With an average of around 10 shows each month, this opportunity marked the beginning of my foray into the realm of professional acting. Over a period, Prasad and I did about a hundred plus shows of the play in various parts of Maharashtra.

As I dedicated myself to honing my craft and delivering my best in the architectural office as a draughtsman, my efforts did not go unnoticed. I was rewarded with a promotion from draughtsman to interior designer and a well-deserved raise in my pay, a testament to my hard work and commitment. Transitioning from a modest monthly income of four hundred rupees a steady raise to four thousand rupees not only provided a financial boost but also validated my skills and dedication.

This pivotal moment in my journey reflected the recognition of my talent and paved the way for further growth and success in my emerging career as an actor.

Life and destiny have a way of testing our approach and resilience as we navigate the ups and downs of our journeys. Challenges, setbacks, and uncertainties often serve as a litmus test of our character, beliefs, and actions. Through these trials, we are given opportunities to demonstrate our adaptability, strength, and capacity for growth.

The obstacles and hurdles that life presents can test our resolve, forcing us to confront our fears, limitations, and insecurities. How we choose to respond to these tests—whether with courage, perseverance, or grace— can shape our path forward and define the outcomes we ultimately experience.

By staying resilient, open-minded, and true to our values in the face of life's trials, we not only navigate challenges more effectively but also uncover hidden strengths and discover new possibilities for growth and transformation. Embracing these tests as opportunities for personal and spiritual development can lead to profound insights, resilience, and a deeper understanding of ourselves and the world around us.

Entering challenging or unfamiliar situations often exposes us to the darker aspects of life or human nature that we may not have encountered before. These metaphorical "dens" can represent environments or circumstances where we are confronted with difficulties, hardships, or moral complexities.

As we navigate these darker and more shadowy aspects of life, we gain a deeper understanding of the complexities and struggles that exist within ourselves and in the world around us. Confronting these "dark sides" can be uncomfortable and unsettling, yet it is often through these experiences that we grow, learn, and develop greater empathy, resilience, and wisdom.

By acknowledging and engaging with the darker aspects of life, we uncover valuable insights, confront our vulnerabilities, and learn to navigate challenges with greater insight and understanding. While these encounters may be daunting, they can ultimately lead to personal growth, increased self-awareness, and a more nuanced perspective on the complexities of the human experience.

The professional theatre industry of yesteryears presented a stark contrast to the glamorous facade it projected from the outside. Once immersed in this world, the reality became evident—it revolved solely around commercial logistics. The payment was contingent on the strength of bookings; for a weak turnout, remuneration was meagre or non-existent. Expecting additional compensation for a sold-out show was deemed unreasonable, almost forbidden.

Travelling to different cities for performances became a harrowing experience. Stars were accorded the luxury of sleeping while we, the supporting actors, found ourselves relegated to the narrow gaps between seats. Post-show, the contrast was stark—stars relished drinks and special cuisine, revelling in relaxation, while we lingered in the shadows, awaiting our turn with unfulfilled longing. The disparity in treatment served as a stark reminder of the hierarchy and uneven dynamics within the industry.

Can I call it the right place at the right time? Maybe or maybe not, but that was the reality of my journey. This endeavour also hampered my stable job in the architecture office. I was unable to give my 100 percent. Finally, my boss found the excuse that I was not qualified as an interior designer and asked me to look for another job. The outcome was quitting my good job in 1985.

I was no less than any of the qualified architects around. In fact, some of my designs were published in the interior design magazine "Inside Outside." I remember my father's advice -

Complete your education gracefully; you will survive in any adverse condition.

While being in the right place at the right time can present opportunities, it is often not sufficient on its own to guarantee success or desired outcomes. Additional factors such as preparation, persistence, skills, and proactive action play crucial roles in capitalising on opportune moments. While the timing of events can indeed be significant, success often hinges on a combination of factors, including readiness, proactive effort, and also luck factor.

The luck factor, often seen as the influence of chance or fortune on outcomes, can play a role in various aspects of life. Luck is commonly associated with unexpected or fortuitous events that bring about favourable results or opportunities.

Luck can present unforeseen opportunities or situations that lead to positive outcomes, such as chance meetings, fortunate circumstances, or unexpected windfalls.

Being in the right place at the right time, with a component of luck, can open doors to favourable opportunities or outcomes that may not have been possible otherwise.

Luck can also be seen in how individuals respond to adversity or challenges. Those who view setbacks as temporary and persist in the face of obstacles may be seen as "lucky" in their ability to bounce back from difficult situations.

Luck is often a matter of perception. What some may attribute to luck, others may see as a result of hard work, preparation, or a positive mindset.

At times, luck can be purely random, with unpredictable events shaping outcomes in ways that defy explanation or control.

While luck can certainly play a role in certain outcomes, combining it with qualities such as preparedness, resilience, and proactive effort can lead to a more holistic approach to achieving success. Balancing the influence of luck with proactive steps and a positive mindset can help individuals make the most of both fortunate opportunities and challenging situations.

I have had quite a journey in the entertainment industry. I performed in 100 shows of "Tour Tour" in a supporting role, hoping to make my mark in the spotlight. However, despite my training and not-so-bad looks, I was continually overlooked for the lead role. As the main lead actors moved on and new faces replaced them, I found myself stuck in the same supporting position.

One day, I mustered the courage to ask the director why I wasn't considered for bigger roles. His response hit me hard - he said I lacked "face value," leaving me speechless.

The term "face value" is often used in the entertainment industry to refer to an individual's perceived marketability or attractiveness to audiences. It goes beyond just talent and skill, encompassing factors like looks, charisma, and overall appeal on screen or stage. When someone is told they lack "face value," it implies that they may not have the physical attributes or qualities that are typically associated with leading roles or garnering audience attention. This feedback can be disheartening for performers who feel they have the talent but are judged primarily on superficial characteristics.

Unable to accept this judgement, I made the tough decision to walk away from the play, uncertain of what the future held.

Leaving behind my architecture job, I delved into the world of television production, accepting a role as an assistant director. The transition came with a significant income drop, from four thousand rupees to a mere three hundred rupees per episode. Despite the financial hardship, I threw myself into the new role, spending countless hours in the producer's office, handling paperwork and planning.

The struggle was real, but my determination to learn and grow in this new medium kept me going. Every moment spent behind the scenes was a step towards honing my skills and understanding the intricacies of television production. It wasn't just about learning; it was about survival. One meal taken care of meant another day to chase my dreams.

My journey has been filled with ups and downs, setbacks, and triumphs. Through it all, I've discovered a resilience within myself and a drive to push forward despite the challenges. This narrative reflects the rollercoaster ride that is the pursuit of passion in the face of adversity.

I found myself at a crucial crossroads in my journey when I crossed paths with a producer named Manju Singh, the sole owner of a company named Tempest Films. It's impossible for me to continue my story honestly without acknowledging her influence. Meeting someone like her was a defining moment that significantly impacted my path. Individuals such as Manju Singh have the power to shape the trajectories of aspiring artists and professionals in the industry. Her presence in my life marked a turning point, opening up new opportunities and perspectives that I had yet to explore. Reflecting on my journey, I recognise the profound impact that encountering producer Manju Singh had on my narrative and the choices I made moving forward.

I had the privilege of collaborating on numerous projects with Manju Singh, ranging from TV serials to short and documentary films. Each endeavour demanded relentless dedication, and I worked tirelessly, pouring my heart and soul into ensuring the success of every project under her guidance. Manju acknowledged my hard work and provided unwavering support throughout our collaborations. Between projects, she even introduced me to feature film directors, broadening my horizons within the industry.

Manju was a producer who exuded intelligence yet possessed a kind heart. While she wasn't overly generous with my remuneration, she made up for it by connecting me with other producers and directors, ensuring that I remained consistently engaged in work. I vividly recall the impactful advice she imparted to me, "It's very easy to enter this industry, but exceedingly tough to stay afloat. While some say that being a jack of all trades hinders success, I urge you to embrace versatility. Become a voracious learner, and you'll find lasting fulfilment in this industry."

Her words resonated deeply with me, serving as a guiding light as I navigated the complexities of the entertainment world. Manju's wisdom not only encouraged me to diversify my skills but also instilled in me the belief that continuous learning and adaptability are key to long-term success in this ever-evolving industry.

During that enchanting period of nearly four to five years, my life was enriched by a series of profound encounters and experiences.

I can't help but reminisce about the unforgettable journey intertwined with the film 'Chowkidar', a cinematic gem brought to life by the vision of producer Manju Singh and the directorial prowess of Canadian filmmaker Domenic Watson. This poignant film, a brainchild of the Ministry of Information, served as a beacon of enlightenment, shedding light on the plight of historical monuments defaced by thoughtless acts of vandalism.

At the helm of this cinematic endeavour stood renowned actors Om Puri and Sutapa Sikdar, with Om Puri portraying the role of a diligent 'chowkidar' tasked with safeguarding a monument and meticulously erasing the graffiti that marred its walls each night. The narrative unfolded against the backdrop of the majestic Jehangir Palace in Orchha, Madhya Pradesh, chosen as the evocative setting for our cinematic canvas. As the production manager entrusted with overseeing all logistical intricacies, it was my privilege to ensure the seamless execution of this cinematic endeavour, bringing to life the powerful message and artistic vision of 'Chowkidar' amidst the historical grandeur of our chosen location.

The year was 1992, a time when cell phones had not yet made their way into the hands of every individual in India. I stood on location in Orchha, diligently arranging lodging and boarding for the film unit set to arrive in two days. Little did I know that a peculiar request was about to turn the tides of our production.

One fine day, in the quaint surroundings of the hotel, I received a trunk call from none other than Manju Singh, the mastermind producer behind our cinematic venture. The request was as bizarre as it was intriguing - to arrange hundreds and thousands of live bats for a pivotal opening shot in the film. In an era devoid of fancy special effects, the challenge was to capture the spectacle of bats swarming out as the grand gates of the palace swung wide open.

With unwavering energy and zeal, I set out on an adventurous quest to fulfil this unique task. Local whispers led me to a nearby tribal village, where the prospect of finding live bats seemed improbable until a revelation unfolded. The locals initially mistook my inquiry for a desire to feast on bat meat, but upon clarifying my intent for the film shoot, a man divulged a startling secret about the palace.

He revealed that beneath the majestic facade of the Jehangir Palace lay a labyrinth of underground chambers, six storeys deep, concealed from the casual observer. In a twist of fate, he offered to assist me in securing the elusive bats under the conditions of financial exchange and a curious request for all the deceased bats that I could gather.

As the clock ticked closer to the impending arrival of the film unit, a race against time commenced. With only a day at my disposal, the stage was set for a rendezvous that would determine the success of our ambitious endeavour. The enigmatic promise of unearthed secrets and the pursuit of elusive creatures cast a mysterious allure over our cinematic voyage, culminating in a rendezvous shrouded in intrigue and whispered legends of subterranean realms waiting to be unveiled.

As the first rays of dawn pierced the morning sky, I stood poised for an unparalleled adventure - a descent into the uncharted depths of the underground palace, a realm shrouded in mystery and untouched by human footprints saved for the tribal guides who led the way. Clad in borrowed attire reminiscent of an astronaut on a lunar mission - a helmet with visor, a leather jacket, hand gloves, tall boots, and double denim jeans layered for protection - I awaited the unfolding of an expedition unlike any other.

At the stroke of seven, three tribal emerged, their bare bodies from the bushes, obscured by a single bedsheet, cane baskets in hand, their essence redolent of ancient wisdom. With solemnity and purpose, they ushered me towards the palace's rear, where an official awaited our party. With practised ease, the portal to the subterranean world swung open, revealing an abyss cloaked in darkness and intrigue.

With silent determination, we ventured forth, my heart a drumbeat in anticipation as we plunged into the abyss. The initial steps led us deeper and deeper, the air growing stale and the darkness enveloping us in a suffocating embrace. My enthusiasm waned as unease crept in, the uneven steps beneath my feet a treacherous path into the unknown. Clutching onto the guide in a blind procession, each step echoed a silent plea for safety in the face of the unseen.

In the stifling dark, punctuated only by the occasional flicker of torchlight, a chilling query escaped my lips, breaking the eerie silence: "Are there any serpents or creatures lurking within these shadows?" The guide's cryptic response, a mixture of reassurance and foreboding, only served to heighten my trepidation. The whispered promise that "They will move away when they hear our footsteps, not to worry" coiled primal fear within me.

As we descended further into the abyss, the weight of the unknown bore down upon me, a palpable sense of dread enveloping my every step. The guide's assurance that our destination lay just beyond, two flights below, offered a sliver of hope amidst the consuming darkness. With a heart heavy with apprehension, I made a harrowing decision to halt in my tracks, beseeching them to forge ahead, urging my spirit to steel itself for the uncharted perils that lay ahead.

As the tribal guides receded into the murky depths, their caution echoing faintly in the darkness, I stood alone, enveloped by a suffocating blackness that seemed to swallow the very essence of light. The cavernous silence pressed in, a heavy shroud that veiled my surroundings in impenetrable obscurity. Adhering to their advice, I brushed against the cold stone wall, my fingertips seeking solace in its unyielding surface as my heartbeat thundered in my ears.

In the oppressive stillness, a subtle shift disrupted the air - a faint rustling, like whispers of unseen wings stirring in the abyss. Suddenly, an otherworldly cacophony shattered the silence, the eerie symphony of a thousand fluttering wings ushering in a maelstrom of chaos. The darkness became alive with frenzied motion, a torrent of shrieking bats swirling around me in a frenetic dance, their invisible forms brushing against my skin with ghostly fervour.

The haunting squeaks and flurried wings created a visceral onslaught, an onslaught of terror and awe that seized my senses, rendering me a captive in this phantasmagorical nightmare. For what felt like an eternity - though in reality mere moments - I stood transfixed amidst this flurry of winged creatures, their frenzied passage like a banshee's wail echoing in the cavernous expanse. Each fleeting brush of their leathery wings against my back sent shivers down my spine, an unforgettable encounter with the primal forces of nature unfurling in the heart of the underground domain.

Those brief but harrowing minutes etched themselves into the fabric of my memory, a vivid tableau of fear and wonder interwoven in the tapestry of my experiences. The darkness held secrets untold, and in that fleeting encounter with the swirling horde of bats, I confronted a surreal phantasm that transcended the boundaries of reality, leaving an indelible mark upon the depths of my consciousness.

Emerging from the stygian depths with baskets teeming with nocturnal creatures shrouded in secrecy, we ascended into the pale light of dawn, our cargo bearing the silent weight of unearthly companions. The tribal wisdom echoing in my ears remained a stark directive - shield these fragile denizens of the dark from the harsh glare of light until the pivotal moment of unveiling.

As the sun painted the sky in hues of anticipation, the moment of reckoning arrived. Jehangir Chaudhary, the master of shadows and light, positioned his camera for the divine spectacle that awaited. Alongside my comrades, we stood poised, the baskets a testament to our audacious foray into the realm of the unknown. In the simmering tension of expectation, the director's call to action pierced the air like a clarion call, signalling the commencement of a momentous event.

With a flick of the hand, the basket's lid unveiled a pandemonium of wings unfurling into the sky, a torrent of bats soaring forth in a symphony of unfettered freedom. The director's vision unfurled before us, the ancient door groaning under the weight of history and mystery as the living shadows took flight into the ethereal morning light. Applause erupted, a thunderous ovation heralding the triumphant culmination of our laborious endeavour.

As a swell of pride washed over me, invigorated by the acclaim of my peers, I turned to the director, a question of satisfaction poised on my lips. Yet, his enigmatic reply, a mere whisper intertwined with mischief, struck a chord of disbelief within me. "Yes," he intoned, his eyes alight with ambition, "but can we have one more shot?"

Aghast and bewildered, my expression mirrored a tumultuous maelstrom of emotions - incredulity mingled with amusement, embarking on the precipice of the absurd and the extraordinary. In that moment of unforeseen challenge and daring request, the fabric of reality seemed to warp and waver, propelling us into a realm where the line between audacity and madness blurred into an iridescent horizon of infinite possibilities.

The valuable lesson learned was that exceeding expectations not only raises the bar for seniors but also cultivates faith and trust in your abilities. By demonstrating a willingness to go above and beyond, you provide assurance that you are willing to push boundaries for the success of the project. This extra effort not only garners respect but also establishes a foundation of reliability and dedication that can lead to greater opportunities and responsibilities.

The pressure peaked when the Director's insistence on a helicopter shot for the film's climactic end thrust us into a daunting conundrum. Approaching me with a sense of desperation, my producer relayed the gravity of the situation, her voice tinged with worry and urgency.

"Sandeep, we're in a bind," she implored, her eyes betraying a mix of anxiety and helplessness. "Domenic is adamant about the helicopter shot as the film's finale. I've exhausted all avenues trying to dissuade him, but he's resolute. He's turned to you for a solution, but you know we lack the necessary budget for such a grand endeavour." With a heavy heart, all I could offer was a solemn promise: "Let me see what I can do."

Throughout the long night that followed, my mind wrestled with the weight of the Director's demand and the financial constraints we faced. In the depths of contemplation, a spark of inspiration ignited within me as a familiar visage resurfaced in my thoughts - Colonel Mehebubani, the commanding officer of the army helicopter base in Zansi.

Merely days prior, during my official visit to Bhopal and Zansi for the acquisition of crucial permission papers, a fateful encounter unfolded with Colonel Mehebubani, the esteemed in charge of the army helicopter base. My stay at the army base of the Western Command in Bhopal was orchestrated as a gesture of hospitality befitting a special guest, courtesy of Manju Singh's influential uncle, the Chief Commander of the Western Command.

In the convivial ambience of the army officers' mess, adorned in my sleek formal attire and polished black shoes, Colonel Mehebubani initially mistook me for a fellow army compatriot due to my demeanour. However, as our conversation unfolded, his intrigue piqued upon learning of my affiliation with the film unit, eliciting a wave of excitement as he delved into avid discussion about the world of cinema. In a serendipitous turn, amidst our exchange, he revealed his wife's profound admiration for the legendary Om Puri, sparking a flicker of inspiration within me.

Seizing upon this connection and recognising a potential path to resolve our dilemma, I resolved to venture to Zansi to seek his assistance in procuring the elusive helicopter shot for the film, recognising the intertwined threads of fate and fortune that led me to this pivotal juncture.

Determined and hopeful, I embarked on an early morning journey to Zansi, where I sought out Colonel Mehebubani in his quarters. Presenting my predicament with a sense of urgency, I articulated the pressing need for assistance to secure the elusive helicopter shot for the film. To my immense relief, Colonel Mehebubani, in his characteristic calm demeanour, unhesitatingly extended his support, offering a glimmer of hope in the face of our daunting challenge.

Following a fruitful discussion, we adjourned for a sumptuous lunch prepared by his skilled 'Khansama', an experience that not only nourished the body but also fostered a sense of camaraderie and warmth. Engaging in spirited conversation with Mrs Mehebubani, I found myself enveloped in a welcoming aura, basking in the shared hospitality and goodwill of the moment.

As our interactions unfolded and the camaraderie strengthened, a pivotal moment emerged when Colonel Mehebubani's orderly arrived with paperwork requiring my signature. With a swell of pride and gratitude, I affixed my signature as the producer representing Manju Singh, a pivotal step that propelled us closer to realising our cinematic vision. Facilitated by the Colonel's adept handling and the simplification of official processes, our task was not only streamlined but infused with a sense of collaboration and shared purpose, underscoring the transformative power of alliances forged through mutual respect and understanding.

With a mix of trepidation and gratitude, I tentatively posed the question to Colonel Mehebubani, "Will there be a cost involved in this incredible favour?" A hearty laugh erupted from the Colonel's lips, dispelling my concerns as he unveiled a whimsical request that stirred a blend of excitement and anticipation within me. "No payment required," he declared with a twinkle in his eye, "just a special dinner at our residence, graced by the presence of Om Puri ji, your producer, and director."

Eagerly agreeing to this unconventional arrangement, I departed for Orchha, my heart buoyed by the promise of a dazzling culmination of our cinematic venture. As the fateful day of the shoot dawned, the air crackled with electric anticipation, the clock ticking inexorably towards the appointed hour of seven in the morning.

Right on schedule, Colonel Mehebubani, accompanied by his wife and a cadre of ground staff, materialised at the palace gates, each step infusing the moment with gravity and significance. An extra jeep whisked away the camera crew - director, DOP, and attendant - to Zansi to prepare the camera rig for the impending aerial spectacle, while Mrs Mehebubani facilitated a convivial gathering with Om Puri ji, Sutapa Sikdar, and Manju Singh, enveloping the courtyard in a tapestry of camaraderie.

At precisely 10.30 am, a message reverberated through the air, signalling the imminent arrival of the chopper. Actors assumed their designated positions under the meticulous direction of DOP Jehangir Chaudhary, the tension mounting with each passing second. At 10.36 am, the deafening roar of the helicopter shattered the tranquillity, prompting us to seek refuge in nearby structures as it soared overhead, executing a breathtaking aerial dance around the palace in a mesmerising whirl of motion and sound.

As the chopper concluded its four exhilarating rounds and departed for Zansi once more, a collective sigh of relief and exhilaration swept through the courtyard. We had captured a breathtaking shot - a triumph of cinematic artistry and ingenuity, a gift bestowed upon us by the benevolence of Colonel Mehebubani, a testament to the boundless possibilities that arise when collaboration, vision, and fortuitous alliances converge in a symphony of creative magic.

Today, these types of shots have become so easy with drones and a minimum crew, but the excitement 'we' experienced was out of this world.

Life can indeed feel like a complex game of hide and seek, where we constantly search for meaning, purpose, and connection amidst the twists and turns of our journey. Just like in the game, there are moments of anticipation, surprise, and uncertainty as we navigate through challenges and opportunities. Sometimes, the things we seek seem to elude us, requiring patience and perseverance to uncover. Other times, life's treasures reveal themselves when we least expect it, adding a touch of magic to the chase.

As we move through the intricate dance of hiding and seeking in life, we learn, grow, and evolve, discovering new facets of ourselves and the world around us. It's a game that requires us to be both active participants and keen observers, ready to embrace the surprises and overcome the obstacles that come our way. And just like in any game, the journey itself holds value, teaching us valuable lessons, building resilience, and shaping our character as we strive to find our place and purpose in this grand adventure called life.

On the day Bhagyashree and I decided to officially get engaged, a whirlwind of emotions and obligations engulfed me. Her parents were still not confident about me. It was quite natural as, like any other father, Dr Vishwas Mehendale had personally seen my days of struggle. He too came from a very modest family and achieved success in life. That was the main reason I told Bhagyashree on the day I proposed to her that if her parents have even the slightest hesitation for our relationship, we will not go ahead in our partnership bonding. Fortunately, the Mehendale family was broad-minded and agreed to our proposal. I too assured them I would excel all my limits to keep their daughter happy. Finally, our engagement ceremony was fixed.

The ceremony was scheduled for the evening, with only a handful of close relatives in attendance. However, I found myself entangled in a web of conflicting duties.

While I was shooting as the chief assistant for the film "Subaha ka Bhoola" with esteemed director Ketan Mehta, my engagement day arrived. This was my second project with Ketan Mehta. Earlier, I worked with him on a commercial film project 'Hero Hiralal' and proved my capacities very well to him, rising from third assistant to first assistant. The weight of commitment bore heavily on my shoulders, and I steadfastly believed in honouring my professional responsibilities first and foremost.

Anticipating that the shoot would conclude by lunchtime, I hoped to make it to my engagement on time. Alas, the lead actor's untimely arrival delayed the proceedings, shattering my plans. As the hours passed, anxiety gnawed at me, for there were no mobile phones in 1988 to hastily inform my beloved Bhagyashree of the unforeseen delay. The thought of her waiting, unaware of my predicament, tugged at my heartstrings.

Unable to focus on the shoot, my mind wandered to the engagement venue where our future together awaited us. The turmoil of being torn between professional duty and a personal milestone gripped me, casting a shadow of doubt and suspense over the day's unfolding events. With no means to alter the course at the last moment, the clock ticked relentlessly as I grappled with the profound choice before me.

Navigating the labyrinth of responsibility and passion, I found myself at a crossroads where the echoes of commitment clashed with the whispers of love and devotion. In this crescendo of conflicting fates, the essence of sacrifice and determination carved a path through the storm, illuminating the intricate dance of life's complex web.

Absolutely, losing focus can lead to making mistakes. When our attention drifts or we become distracted, our ability to complete tasks accurately and efficiently diminishes. Whether it's due to external distractions, lack of motivation, or a cluttered mind, losing focus can result in errors, oversight, or missed opportunities. Maintaining concentration and being fully present in the task at hand is key to minimising mistakes and achieving desired outcomes.

In a moment of realisation, I found myself facing a critical error in continuity during the filming of a scene, a misstep that slipped past my attention until the completion of the shot. With a sense of profound regret, I mustered the courage to approach Director Ketan, owning up to my mistake with a sense of humility and embarrassment. The weight of the error loomed over me, knowing that time was of the essence for both of us.

In the tense aftermath of my critical mistake on the final day of the shoot, Director Ketan's piercing question in a very soft tone reverberated through me, cutting through the turmoil in me like a sharp blade. "What happened, Sandeep? How could you let this happen, especially on the last day?" His tone held a hint of disappointment and urgency, igniting a swarm of regret within me.

To my surprise, Ketan's response was one of unexpected grace and understanding. He did not erupt in anger or reprimand me, but instead, he met my confession with a sense of calm and wisdom. Ketan's belief that 'We are humans and bound to make mistakes' resonated deeply within me. He understood that mistakes are often a part of the creative process, acknowledging that genuine errors arise from human lapses rather than ill intent.

In that moment of vulnerability and acceptance, I learned a valuable lesson in humility and accountability. Ketan's compassionate response not only alleviated my fears but also instilled in me a sense of grace and forgiveness towards myself. Through his guidance, I embraced the notion that forgiveness and growth stem from acknowledging our fallibility, paving the way for genuine learning and progress in both craft and character.

With a heavy heart and a voice barely above a whisper, I managed to croak out, "Sir... I am deeply sorry." Each word hung heavily in the air, laden with the weight of my error and the consequences that loomed ahead.

As the gravity of the situation settled around us, Ketan's unexpected response broke through the tension like a ray of light in a storm. "No problem, we'll shoot it again. I'll speak to the location manager for extra hours," he declared with a sense of calm authority that quelled the rising panic within me. Annu Kapoor, the lead actor, extended a reassuring hand of support, offering solace in a moment of chaos.

"Extra hours..." The words echoed in my mind, triggering a tumultuous whirlwind of images and emotions. Flickers of a potential showdown at Bhagyashree's home, her father's disapproving glare, and her mix of anger and desolation danced before me like vivid scenes from a harrowing drama. The weight of failure and the fear of consequences bore down on me, painting a haunting picture of what could unravel in the wake of my mistake.

In this crucible of heightened emotions and looming challenges, the prospect of a reshoot held the key to redemption, not just on the screen but in the intricate web of relationships and obligations that defined my existence. The stage was set for a pivotal moment of reckoning, where the lines between professional duty and personal life blurred, creating a canvas of uncertainty and transformation.

As the clock's hands crept towards 2:00 pm, a sense of mounting tension gripped me. Director Ketan, ever perceptive, noticed my internal turmoil and approached me with a gentle inquiry, "What is it, Sandeep? Is everything alright?"

In a hushed voice barely above a whisper, I mustered the courage to disclose my pressing truth, "Sir... I am getting engaged today... in just a few hours... today."

Ketan's exclamation resonated through the set like a thunderclap, his words ringing out with a mix of surprise and celebration. The atmosphere instantly transformed as congratulations and well-wishes poured in from all directions, enveloping me in a whirlwind of support and camaraderie.

With a light-hearted remark that lifted the weight off my shoulders, Ketan's jovial response reverberated through the set, "That's a big problem, brother! You are out for committing another big mistake." Laughter rippled through the crew as Ketan playfully ushered me towards the door, announcing to all, "Now, before I kick your butt, scoot off and have fun."

Puzzled yet relieved by the unexpected turn of events and touched by the warmth of their good wishes, I expressed my gratitude to everyone before almost sprinting towards the exit. In that moment of shared joy and understanding, the pressure and uncertainties melted away, leaving behind a trail of anticipation and excitement as I embarked on the next chapter of my journey.

In the whirlwind of emotions and unexpected turns on that pivotal day, a profound truth struck me. Rushing towards my next destination, I couldn't shake off the feeling of being in the right place at the right time.

Director Ketan's supportive words, the cheers from my colleagues, and the sudden wave of well-wishes all seemed to align perfectly, ushering me towards a significant moment. In the midst of juggling work and personal life, chaos and excitement, everything fell into place like a harmonious symphony of fortune and opportunity.

In that fleeting moment of clarity, I realised that life has a way of orchestrating moments of magic and chance, positioning us exactly where we need to be at just the right moment. It was a reminder that amidst the chaos, there exists a deeper harmony when we follow the unexpected rhythms of fate, embracing each twist and turn as a part of our destined journey.

Stepping into my engagement at the right place at the right time, I carried with me a newfound gratitude for the serendipitous nature of life, ready to embrace the challenges and wonders that lay ahead on this grand adventure. It was a stark reminder of the beauty that unfolds when we allow ourselves to be in sync with the flow of the universe, ready to seize the opportunities that come our way.

❖

4

LEARNINGS FROM OTHERS' MISTAKES

In the labyrinth of life, we often find ourselves entangled in the age-old myth that dictates we must 'learn from our mistakes.' But what if I tell you that the true essence of wisdom lies not solely in our own missteps, but in the shadows cast by the mistakes of others that pierce through the veil of our understanding?

Picture a tapestry woven with threads of experience, each strand bearing the mark of fallibility and uncertainty. As we navigate through the intricacies of existence, we encounter the remnants of others' errors strewn along our path, each misstep a cautionary tale whispered by the winds of time.

The myth unravels as we dare to embrace a deeper truth - that the resonating echoes of others' misjudgements, failures, and tribulations resonate with a haunting clarity that transcends the confines of our own limitations. Their stories become waypoints in our narrative, guiding us through treacherous terrain and murky waters with the beacon of hindsight illuminating the way.

So, let us shatter the myth and rewrite the narrative, for in the symphony of shared experiences, the melody of growth and enlightenment reverberates loudest. Let us glean wisdom not only from the scars we bear but from the scars of those who walked before us, for in their missteps lie the keys to unlocking the secrets of resilience, foresight, and transformation.

As we navigate the journey of life, let us not only learn from our mistakes but also bear witness to the invaluable lessons gifted to us by the mistakes of others, addressing a narrative rich in depth, empathy, and the boundless resilience of the human spirit.

In this pivotal chapter of my journey, I stand at the crossroads of introspection and vulnerability, ready to lay bare the raw truth of my missteps. Like a sudden storm shattering the calm facade of order and stability, my mistakes delivered a devastating blow at a time when the dust seemed to settled, leaving me reeling in their turbulent aftermath.

In my experience, particularly within the realm of the film industry, the genesis of mistakes often lies in the realm of overconfidence. The insidious nature of overconfidence manifests gradually over time, elicited by a series of successful outcomes that align with one's intentions. When faced with challenges, overcoming them seamlessly can breed a sense of invincibility, fostering the belief that one is impervious to failure. This distorted perception, fuelled by past triumphs, engenders a dangerous mentality that whispers, "I am capable of conquering any obstacle."

As previously mentioned, one of the significant missteps in my journey towards success was venturing into producing and directing a television serial without attaining a comprehensive understanding of the intricacies involved. This decision, made without complete insight, stands out as a pivotal mistake in my life. Fortunately, the project was funded with my personal resources, sparing me the ignominy of debt repayment and averting a potential financial catastrophe. I take immense pride in acknowledging that despite facing substantial losses, there isn't a single technician or actor who can assert that I failed to honour my commitments and pay them for their services.

As I navigate the landscape of my errors, each misstep feels like a punch to the face, a stark reminder of the fragility of my carefully constructed reality. The veil of complacency is torn asunder, revealing the stark reality of my fallibility and the weight of accountability that rests heavily on my shoulders.

Despite the pain and discomfort that accompany such admissions, I embrace this moment of reckoning with courage and humility. It is in the crucible of acknowledging my faults and owning up to the consequences that true growth and transformation are born. Like the phoenix rising from the ashes of my misjudgements, I am poised to emerge stronger, wiser, and more resilient than before.

As I pen this chapter of transparency and self-reflection, I lay bare my scars and vulnerabilities for all to see, for it is in the act of embracing our imperfections that we pave the way for redemption, learning, and the unwavering pursuit of a better version of ourselves.

During the dawn of the new millennium, my life seemed to align perfectly with the harmonious melody of success and stability serenading me. The prestigious role of heading the films department at Contract Advertising, one of India's esteemed agencies, painted a picture of contentment and accomplishment. The echoes of my past triumphs in filmmaking, coupled with a prosperous tenure as the Film Chief at Triton Communications, had paved the way for this pinnacle, offering a lucrative annual package of seven lakh per annum that spoke of recognition and validation.

In between this pursuit of achievements, I found myself at a fortuitous juncture where dreams transformed into reality.

In the bustling suburbs of Mumbai, my life found solace in an accommodating wife—a rock in times of distress. Our home echoed with the laughter of two precious children: a four-year-old daughter's innocence and a one-year-old boy's mischief. Through their playful energy, our house transformed into a sanctuary of joy and chaos. Amidst our growing family, the acquisition of a house and car symbolised our shared dreams and stability, anchoring us in the whirlwind of parenthood and shared experiences.

With the acquisition of my first car, a proud achievement marking a significant milestone in my journey, a desire stirred within me to share the details of how I procured the necessary funds with my boss. Revealing that a portion was borrowed from my father-in-law, I hoped to showcase my financial prudence and transparency. However, insinuations from colleagues attributing my purchase to illicit gains from external producers began to circulate, casting aspersions on my integrity.

Upon confiding in my boss about the source of funding, expecting recognition for my diligence, I was met with a profound lesson in discretion and professionalism. With sagacity, my boss cautioned, "Your financial decisions are your own, and there is no need to disclose them to me. Guard your personal matters carefully; unwarranted explanations can sow seeds of doubt regarding your integrity." This sage advice underscored the importance of maintaining a boundary between personal affairs and professional interactions, shielding oneself from unwarranted speculation and upholding the trust and credibility crucial in the workplace.

Embarking on a challenging journey from the ground up taught me a fundamental lesson that has since become a guiding principle in my life: always endeavour to be kind and supportive to everyone, and strive to uplift those around you on their path to success. My own experience of starting from scratch instilled in me a deep appreciation for the significance of lending a helping hand and fostering a spirit of generosity towards others.

By extending support and assistance to others in their endeavours, we not only spread positivity and goodwill but also contribute to the collective growth and prosperity of our community. Empowering someone to build their ladder of success, whether through mentorship, guidance, or a simple act of encouragement, not only enriches their journey but also fosters a culture of collaboration and mutual benefit.

Our agency had landed the prestigious opportunity to create a major commercial for Warner Lambert, renowned for their successful brand Chiclets in the market. Our team crafted a captivating concept for the Chiclets brand commercial, which resonated with the client. Among the top production houses, Highlight was selected to bring this vision to life, with the esteemed Mahesh Mathai leading the project as director and cinematographer.

In the midst of this typical scenario of clients pushing for results as if they were due yesterday, the entire Highlight Production team found themselves involved in a shoot in Jaipur, not expected back for another fifteen days. With the pressure mounting and clients unable to adjust their marketing deadlines, the responsibility of delivering the final product fell heavily on my shoulders as the film chief. Feeling the weight of the situation, my only recourse was to turn to Mahesh Mathai for help.

Approaching Mahesh, I emphasised the urgency of the situation, explaining that the fate of my job hung in the balance. Known for his genuine nature and flexibility, Mahesh faced his own challenges as his regular production team was unavailable. Desperate for a solution, I implored Mahesh to see past our agency-client roles and view me as a member of his production team, offering to assist in any way necessary. After thoughtful consideration, Mahesh agreed to collaborate, reaching out to his contacts like Prasoon Pandey and Abhinay Deo, both now prominent figures in the industry as producers and directors. Thanks to Mahesh's gracious understanding and willingness to adapt, work was swiftly commissioned, marking a pivotal moment in our journey towards meeting the demanding client expectations.

At one point, we faced challenges with the casting of the lead character. The creatives were dissatisfied at times, and Mahesh expressed his discontent on other occasions. I asked Mahesh to give me a detailed brief of the character he was looking for so that I could check and try to find someone from the theatre. Mahesh shared his directorial vision of the character, and I started thinking.

By offering help and support to others in their pursuits, we not only promote positivity and goodwill but also aid in the advancement and prosperity of our community as a whole. Empowering individuals on their path to success through support, guidance, and encouragement not only enriches their experience but also nurtures a collaborative atmosphere yielding mutual benefits.

I remembered a young actor I had met during one of the shows of 'Tour Tour'. His talent and humble nature left a lasting impression on me. Keen to support his journey in the industry, I promptly contacted him and invited him to my office for a meeting. The next morning, he arrived punctually, displaying his professionalism, which I greatly appreciated, and warmly greeted him.

"Hello! I am Atul Parchure... And you are? Sandeep Kashyap?"

"Yes, please be seated. I know you very well, but we haven't met formally before."

I explained to him why I called him and proposed that he should take on this role. He was also interested in doing it.

Finally, I asked him, "What are your expectations regarding honorarium?"

"I have never done an ad film before, so I seriously don't know what the normal payment is." Atul was very modest. I knew very well what our budget was for this main casting, yet I wanted to hear from him so that he would feel good.

"I sincerely don't have any idea about the payments in advertising. You only guide me." Atul was lenient in admitting this ignorance.

"You work on the professional stage. If you don't mind, may I ask how much they pay you per show?" I asked him a direct question.

"Three hundred and fifty rupees per show," promptly answered Atul without any hesitation. I liked his honesty.

"Will it be okay if we pay you an honorarium of a hundred shows for a one-day shoot on next Sunday? I mean thirty-five thousand rupees?"

For a moment, Atul was quiet and just looking at me. I thought either he was not believing me or might be thinking of asking for something more. To my surprise, Atul was thinking about his drama show which was scheduled for the next Sunday.

"I have committed to a show next Sunday at four thirty PM in Ghatkopar, about one hour from Ballard Estate where you intend to shoot." Atul was seriously worried about his commitment. I had no words for his sincerity towards commitment. I promised him that I would ensure that I make all arrangements for him so that he can meet his commitment.

The shoot unfolded seamlessly, with Atul delivering an exceptional performance that captivated all present. As the cameras ceased their endless whirring and the lights dimmed, a special car whisked Atul away to his awaiting stage in Ghatkopar, ensuring his punctuality for the drama show.

But the twists of fate did not halt there. In a stroke of luck, Prasoon Pandey, who was helping his friend Mahesh Mathai extend his generosity, unveiled another grand opportunity for Atul - a lucrative project set amidst the enchanting landscapes of Russia. As Atul embarked on a journey to America for yet another venture, he found himself not just another face in the crowd but the beloved "Chiclet boy," garnering recognition and admiration wherever he roamed, penning autographs for eager fans along the way. Such was the dramatic metamorphosis of a humble actor, catapulted into the limelight of success and adulation.

Assisting others is undoubtedly a noble and commendable act, reflective of empathy, kindness, and a desire to make a positive impact on someone's life. However, it is crucial to recognise that the essence of helping others lies in the selfless intent to offer support, guidance, or care without expecting anything tangible in return. While many individuals may express gratitude or reciprocate the kindness shown to them, it is important to acknowledge that not everyone may acknowledge or appreciate the help they receive.

Atul's exceptional nature shone through when, as he ascended to stardom, he openly shared the aforementioned incident in a public interview, graciously expressing gratitude towards me. Despite Atul's acknowledgement, some individuals from Highlight insinuated that my noble deed was motivated by ulterior motives, casting a shadow of doubt over the purity of my actions. This misunderstanding and questioning of my intentions remain a source of regret for me.

Understanding that not all acts of kindness may be openly acknowledged underscores the importance of humility and altruism. By embracing the notion of selfless giving, individuals can cultivate a sense of fulfilment derived from the act itself rather than external validation. Ultimately, the beauty of helping others lies in the purity of the gesture, enriching both the giver and the recipient, irrespective of whether the *favour is openly recognised or not.*

It was amidst this backdrop of recognition and ambition that I crossed paths with a dynamic production enthusiast, Avinash Chowgule, who was a line producer and wanted to become a big fish in the market. His zeal and hunger for success were a striking contrast to the tranquillity of my settled life.

His relentless pursuit of materialistic success ignited a spark within my ambitious soul, planting the seed of aspiration even deeper in the fertile grounds of my psyche. As the tides of change ebbed and flowed, my role transitioned into one of bridging creative visions with client expectations, orchestrating the symphony of collaboration and execution to ensure satisfaction across all fronts.

In this pivotal moment of convergence, where ambition danced with opportunity and the hunger for more gnawed at the edges of contentment, a transformative journey beckoned, promising a path filled with risks, rewards, and the unwavering pursuit of excellence in the ever-evolving landscape of advertising and creativity.

During that era, Ad filmmakers were treated as supreme creative crusaders. Their budgets were untouched, and their showreels were revered as the ultimate yardstick of success. However, my first misstep came when I dared to question the unchallenged norms by demanding budget breakdowns. Well-versed in the intricacies of filmmaking rates and standards, I aimed to shed light on the nebulous realm of logistics that often lurked behind the glittering facade of creativity.

Presenting my case to my superiors, I boldly stated that I could produce the same ad film at a twenty-five percent reduced cost compared to the inflated figures touted by the so-called 'reputed' producer-directors. While some pondered the possibility, others branded me a fool or accused me of ulterior motives looking for an excuse to seek kickbacks. Amidst the sceptics, one producer-director even dared to tempt me with a fifteen percent cut, which I graciously accepted by subtracting the agreed percentage from his inflated budgeted amount. I humbly admit that I did receive monetary assistance from one or two producers, yet the weight of my conscience prevented me from finding peace in my slumber.

My rationale for requesting a budget breakdown was simple: just as you or I would pay the same price to hire a camera from the market, the rates for studio hire, lights, and other essentials remained consistent across the board. There were no special prices for different individuals; the costs were uniform and unchanging even for the technicians (based on their grade and experience). Individual remuneration and creative fees were non-negotiable. This system began to reveal the significant profits made by producers.

The essence of an individual's creativity and ability remains unchallenged and non-negotiable. While the fees requested by an individual may seem unquestionable, a subtle shift in perspective reveals that budgets can often be streamlined to achieve significant savings of twenty-five to thirty-five percent. This optimal balance showcases that innovation and resourcefulness can pave the way for cost-effective solutions without compromising on the quality or impact of the end product.

One day, the President of our company summoned me to his office with an intriguing dilemma. A prestigious client had expressed interest in creating an Ad film, but their budget was meagre. Despite the client's reputation, no producer was willing to undertake the project for such a limited amount. The President turned to me with a challenge: could I find someone willing to take on this unique project?

Here, Avinash Chowgule entered my life. He proposed a very lucrative and sensible proposal.

"Why don't you consider directing the film yourself? I'll take on the role of producer. How much longer will you continue this liaison work? You're putting in tireless efforts to build someone else's future," he remarked pointedly.

"I understand my creative team; they may not view me as a suitable director. They prefer a fancy showreel for validation," I confessed.

"You have to start somewhere. Every journey has a beginning. At least give it a shot. If they refuse, I can seek out budding directors who are eager to take on the job for a modest fee," he urged, his tone unwavering and resolute.

The notion that no one should let go of a significant opportunity carries profound implications for personal and professional growth. Opportunities are like rare gems, presenting themselves at pivotal moments in our lives, offering the potential to propel us towards success, fulfilment, and advancement. Choosing to seize these opportunities, rather than letting them slip through our grasp, can lead to transformative outcomes and open doors to new horizons.

Opportunities often come wrapped in challenges or disguised as risks, requiring courage, determination, and a willingness to step outside comfort zones. By embracing these moments of possibility, individuals can chart new paths, expand their capabilities, and cultivate valuable experiences that shape their future trajectory. Furthermore, *capitalising* on big opportunities can lead to significant personal and professional advancement, unlocking doors to new connections, achievements, and recognition.

In essence, recognising and seizing big opportunities is not just about taking a chance; it's about harnessing the power of possibility to drive meaningful progress and evolution. By refusing to let go of these pivotal moments, individuals can catalyse growth, instigate change, and carve out a future filled with promise, success, and endless potential.

In discussions with my creative team, reactions varied from encouragement to disbelief; some laughed at my audacity for the task ahead. The consensus was unanimous: tackling the project within a one-week timeframe and with a limited budget seemed like an insurmountable challenge. Despite the scepticism and the odds stacked against us, no outside producer was willing to take on the job that I had wholeheartedly agreed to undertake.

Avinash owned a registered production house named OMS Productions, short for "One Man Show Productions." I toiled tirelessly, facing a cascade of challenges that seemed insurmountable. From the relentless Mumbai rains and the disruptions caused by the Ganesh festivals to last-minute changes in the lead model, the hurdles kept mounting. However, the most significant obstacle presented itself in the form of accommodating babies of various ages for a baby product film, each accompanied by mothers dealing with the tantrums and demands that come with the territory.

Amidst the storm of challenges and obstacles, I managed to successfully complete the film within the given budget and timeframe. On the day of the presentation, I stumbled in the client's conference room, my exhaustion evident as I moved like a zombie. To my astonishment, the client loved the film, a rare moment of satisfaction in the realm of creatives, who perpetually seek perfection and more.

As I stood in a daze, my boss acknowledged my hard work, a subtle nod of appreciation in place of the usual embrace. Exiting the conference room, the weight of the ordeal finally caught up with me, and I collapsed under the strain.

The scene transitions abruptly to a hospital room, where I lay confined due to overexertion, a stark reminder of the toll that relentless dedication and unyielding pursuit of success can exact on both body and soul.

After Avinash received the payment, he approached me a week later with disheartening news – we hadn't made a profit on the project, but the loss was manageable. Assuring me to take it easy, he pledged to make amends and ensure recovery in the upcoming project. Placing my trust in his words, I agreed to proceed with his proposed "Next project".

As we awaited our next project, set to begin in about a month, my wife pointed out that I hadn't taken a holiday in nearly two years, and the kids were eager for a getaway. Avinash overheard the conversation and promptly suggested a trip to a hill station in South India. Without hesitation, he offered to book our tickets, assuring me that I could settle the expenses later. Appreciative of the opportunity, I gave him the go-ahead to arrange our travel and accommodation for the much-needed family vacation.

Faith and trust, with their ethereal essence, possess a remarkable ability to cascade through the tapestry of our lives, sometimes overriding the rationality and practicalities that typically govern our decisions and actions. In moments when logic whispers caution, faith and trust emerge as guiding forces, leading us down pathways abundant with uncertainty yet rich with possibilities.

At times, faith and trust beckon us to take leaps of faith to embrace the unknown with unwavering conviction that all will unfold as it should. In these moments, practicality takes a back seat as we surrender to the wisdom of the heart and the serenity of belief. It is in these instances that miracles unfurl, connections deepen, and destinies align in ways that transcend the limitations of practical thinking.

While practicality serves as a beacon of reason in the tumultuous seas of life, faith and trust act as lighthouses guiding us through the storms, illuminating paths we may not have dared to tread. Embracing the transformative power of faith and trust, we unlock doors to unforeseen opportunities, forge unbreakable bonds, and discover the boundless potential that lies within the realm of belief. In this dance between practicality and faith, it is often the latter that propels us towards moments of true magic, where dreams coalesce with reality, and the extraordinary becomes within reach.

Very promptly, Avinash made the bookings for flights and hotels for all of us. I immediately offered him a cheque payment for my share, but he said not to pay him in his name. Instead, he provided me with the name of a supplier who had provided materials for our shoot. I then gave him a bearer cheque in that name.

Our trip was very good. Children also enjoyed it. Our friendship also deepened. The tranquil atmosphere in the mountains was soothing and satisfying. I never imagined that this was the silence before the turmoil. This situation could be an impending storm in an enigmatic veil.

Like the calm surface of a lake before a tempestuous downpour, it was a moment pregnant with tension and unease, a fleeting pause before chaos unfurled its wings.

Upon returning to Mumbai from various sources, I learned that Avinash had made incredible profits on the job, far exceeding my expectations. The set supplier, to whom I had issued the cheque, informed me that Avinash had taken all the money in cash before providing the cheque.

Frustration and anger seethed within me, boiling over at Avinash's casual indifference. It felt as though I was betraying my company by condoning his actions. In a tense meeting with Avinash, I insisted that returning a portion of the excessive profits would demonstrate integrity and goodwill towards the company. It was not just a matter of money but one of respect and trust that could prove invaluable in securing future projects.

Avinash vehemently opposed my suggestion, his disagreement fuelling the flames of our confrontation. Resolute in my stance, I asserted that if he refused, I would withdraw from pitching for the next job. I refused to play a part in a cycle of deceit and opted to seek out a more reputable producer instead, determined to uphold my principles and distance myself from the compromising situation at hand.

There was no interaction between us for a few days. During this tranquil yet deceptive interlude, there was an eerie stillness that belied the storm brewing beneath the surface. It was a moment of suspended animation, one like where the world holds its breath in anticipation of what is to come. The quietude can be deceiving, offering no clues to the turmoil that lurks just beyond the horizon, waiting to shatter the serenity of the moment.

That unforgettable day stands frozen in the recesses of my mind, each vivid detail etched with the sting of betrayal and injustice. Stepping into the familiar office environment, an unsettling sense of foreboding prickled at my skin as Greta's urgent intercom call pierced the air. Her typically warm voice carried a jarring note of gravity, forewarning a storm brewing on the horizon.

Upon entering my boss's cabin, the sight that greeted me was a tableau of incriminating evidence meticulously laid out – photocopies of travel agency invoices, hotel bills, food expenses, and shopping receipts, each piece painting a damning picture of supposed impropriety. The accusatory air wrapped around me like a suffocating cloak as my boss wasted no time levying the grave allegations against me.

Stunned and disoriented, I recounted the events of my hill station trip with Avinash, the pieces of the puzzle clicking into place with painful clarity. What I had initially viewed as a gesture of goodwill from Avinash now morphed into a sinister plot, a trap meticulously set to ensnare me in a web of deceit and false accusations. The realisation of being manipulated and deceived cut deep, sowing seeds of indignation and anger within my soul.

In a crescendo of emotions, I stood before my boss, the weight of his mistrust and the weight of fabricated evidence bearing down on my shoulders like a crushing burden. Challenged with the ultimate question of belief in my integrity, I found myself grappling with a harsh reality – my dedication, sincerity, and loyalty called into question, draining away with each passing moment.

With a heavy heart and a firm resolve born from a wounded spirit, I made a decision that echoed with the finality of a closing chapter. Confronted with baseless accusations and a twisted narrative of deceit, I uttered the fateful words that sealed my fate – a resignation tinged with the bitterness of injustice and a poignant departure from a world that had forsaken me, leaving behind a legacy tarnished with false colours and a heart heavy with the weight of unwarranted shame.

Returning home with a heavy heart, I shared with Bhagyashree the solemn news of my resignation. Without uttering a word, her eyes spoke volumes, absorbing the weight of my turmoil. Seeking solace, I retreated to the sanctuary of my room, allowing tears to flow freely, a silent release of anguish and frustration.

Amid my silent turmoil, a comforting presence approached me, consoling hands gently alighting upon my shoulders. Startled, I turned to meet Bhagyashree's gaze, her eyes reflecting a wellspring of empathy and understanding. In a moment fraught with vulnerability, I implored her, "What have I done wrong? Why must it always be me?"

With quiet strength and unwavering faith, Bhagyashree's voice resonated with an air of reassurance and unwavering belief. "Because you possess a resilience that surpasses all trials. This is but another test, a challenge sent forth by a higher power. I have no doubt that you will emerge triumphant, just as you have done countless times before. In this crucible of adversity, I know you will rise, resolute and resilient, painting the canvas of this trial with the vibrant hues of your unwavering spirit."

Mistakes, often disguised as opportunities, hold profound lessons for growth and self-discovery. By reflecting, seeking feedback, and embracing the learnings they offer, we fortify our resilience and deepen our wisdom. Embracing challenges as disguised gifts, we emerge stronger, wiser, and poised to navigate life's intricacies with renewed clarity and purpose.

Learning from our mistakes should not become a recurring pattern in our lives, as it may lead to a cycle of constantly committing new errors. Through my own experiences, I have gleaned a valuable lesson: instead of focusing solely on self-correction, it is wiser to draw insights from the mistakes of others and proceed with cautious steps. Embracing this wisdom allows us to navigate life with greater awareness, avoiding the pitfalls that come with repeating past errors and harnessing the collective wisdom of those around us to make informed and mindful decisions.

❖

5

PROBLEMS ARE OPPORTUNITIES

Problems often arise as unwelcome guests, casting shadows of doubt and discomfort over our path. Yet, hidden within the folds of adversity lie seeds of opportunity, waiting to be unearthed by those daring enough to perceive challenges as stepping stones to growth and transformation. It is within the realm of problems that the alchemy of resilience and innovation thrives, turning obstacles into gateways to new horizons and solutions. I would like to take you on a journey where problems are not obstacles but rather portals to unexpected possibilities, where each setback is a hidden opportunity waiting to be discovered and embraced. If you can solve them with your gathered knowledge and experience successfully, you attain superiority as a problem solver.

It was during my beautiful and memorable theatre days in 1976 in Goa before coming to Mumbai. We were staging a play "Antigone".

"Antigone" is an Athenian tragedy written by Sophocles in (or before) 441 BC and first performed at the Festival of Dionysus of the same year. We were staging its Marathi version for a prestigious state-level drama competition. Winning an award in this competition was like winning an Oscar for amateur theatre groups.

The play is about Antigone's disobedience of Creon's rules when she insists on burying her brother, Polyneices. To Creon's distress, Antigone, Haemon, and Eurydice die at the end of the play. The play addresses themes of civil disobedience, morality, loyalty, authority, and gender.

The stage was a magnificent blend of elevated platforms and Roman-style pillars, creating a stunning backdrop for our performance. The play began smoothly, with everything building up beautifully towards a crescendo.

However, just a few minutes before the intermission, during a pivotal scene on civil disobedience, disaster struck. One of the pillars at the centre right unexpectedly toppled over.

In an instant, the atmosphere shifted. The audience gasped, and we, the actors on stage, were momentarily frozen in shock. Thankfully, no one was hurt, but for a brief moment, everything seemed to stand still.

As the curtains closed for the interval, tension mounted backstage during a meeting in the green room. Initially, the idea of hastily repositioning the fallen pillar and carrying on with the play was discussed. However, our astute director quickly intervened, cautioning against this course of action. He emphasised that such a move would reveal the mishap to the audience, undermining the illusion of the performance. Instead, he advocated leaving the pillar in its fallen state, stating that if a mistake is made, it is crucial to provide a rationale for it to prevent it from appearing as a mere error. We all agreed, ensured the stability of the other pillars, and continued with the play.

Following the show, we were greeted with a resounding standing ovation from the audience. Many lauded the fallen pillar as a symbolic representation of civil unrest, praising the set designer and stage management for their skilful execution of the theatrical effect. The unexpected twist became a pivotal moment in the performance, elevating the play to new heights. It was this creative ingenuity that ultimately garnered us the award, showcasing how a seemingly disastrous mishap was transformed into a winning element that captivated and resonated with our audience.

It is worth mentioning that despite the success of that particular performance, for subsequent shows, we faced the daunting task of recreating and perfecting the fallen pillar act. The initial spontaneity and novelty of the mishap had to be meticulously replicated with precision and effort to ensure consistency and maintain the impact that had captivated our audience. This challenge underscored the dedication and professionalism of our team, highlighting the behind-the-scenes commitment required to deliver a flawless and compelling production with each subsequent performance.

Another episode of sheer thrill and profound learning marked my journey with my debut film as a Director – "Sane Guruji." After a brief tenure in advertising, I ventured into freelancing in 2003, an endeavour that led to the birth of my modest production house. It was here that I dived into the realms of Ad films, documentaries, and corporate productions.

It was during this exciting phase that I was approached by a group of passionate enthusiasts. They proposed a documentary about the famous Indian freedom fighter, Sane Guruji. The journey of creating this film could fill the pages of a book – a story for another time.

At the outset, I knew little about Sane Guruji, and to complicate matters, the group had no script, no professional experience, and no financial backing. Initially, I was sceptical about taking up the project. But as I delved deeper into researching Sane Guruji, I discovered a compelling and largely forgotten hero whose life cried out for cinematic representation. The filmmaker within me was electrified by his story, and I became determined to bring this unsung patriot to the screen.

I suggested to the team that we should seek government funding to ensure this forgotten hero found his place in the spotlight. They wholeheartedly supported the idea, and to our delight, the government agreed to finance the project.

Our film unit was small, with only three professionally qualified members: myself as the Director, the main lead actor, and the cameraman. The rest were enthusiastic amateurs, driven by a shared passion.

Thus began another thrilling and dramatic chapter in my life, a journey filled with endless learning and unexpected surprises.

The initial jolts I encountered were like relentless waves trying to pull me down, shouting at me to abandon the project. But the more I learned about Sane Guruji, the more captivated I became. His character transformed me from an aggressive, hot-headed individual into a calm, balanced, and rational human being.

With renewed vigour, I plunged into the paperwork and soon had a bound script ready. My producer, in his naivety, suggested we censor the script with the authorities. Any other director might have erupted at such a suggestion, but I remained composed. I calmly explained that films are censored after they're made, not before.

Creating a period film to depict the pre-independence era on screen was a colossal challenge—one that even seasoned production designers would find daunting. To my dismay, the producer recommended his uncle as the production designer, boasting about his skills in decorating Ganesh festival pandals.

I bit my tongue and suppressed my frustration. My inner voice urged me to accept the situation, believing that I could still bring my vision to life. I decided to design everything myself and have the producer's uncle execute the plans. This way, I could ensure that the end result would be as close to my vision as possible.

Thus, began my journey navigating through obstacles with determination and creativity, driven by the inspiring tale of Sane Guruji and the unwavering belief in my own abilities.

We embarked on our shooting adventure with the daunting deadline of completing the entire film in just thirty days. We faced a myriad of challenges: no gaffer, no grips, no qualified costume designer, and not even a dedicated production manager.

Despite these hurdles, our passion and determination drove us forward. The setting was chaotic, but the spirit was electrifying. Each day was a new challenge, a new testing ground for our creativity and resilience. We improvised lighting setups, devised costumes with whatever resources we had at hand, and worked tirelessly to bring the world of pre-independence India to life.

With every scene, the story of Sane Guruji unfolded, and the raw energy and enthusiasm of our makeshift crew shone through. The lack of traditional support systems forced us to innovate and think on our feet, forging a team spirit that was as unyielding as it was inspiring.

We persevered, driven by a common goal: to tell the story of a forgotten hero with authenticity and passion. The odds were stacked against us, but with every shot, we inched closer to our dream, turning every obstacle into an opportunity to prove our mettle.

The journey was far from easy, but it was undoubtedly one of the most exhilarating experiences I'd ever had.

I knew that extracting convincing performances from local, inexperienced actors would be a formidable challenge. Hence, I meticulously divided the scene into short cuts, breaking down each line to ensure that even the smallest details would be captured perfectly. This painstaking preparation consumed a significant amount of time, but I was determined to get it right.

On the day of the shoot, we arrived at the location well ahead of time. I wanted ample time to shortlist six competent actors from the group of fifteen to twenty stage actors expected to show up— Eleven appeared almost two hours late. Out of the eleven, five backed out when they realised that they would have to shave their heads. I was left with seven, somehow convinced by the producer. Out of the seven, one was absolutely incompetent, but I was compelled to retain him as he was the local coordinator's relative. It was going to feel like a last-minute screen test in the midst of our tight schedule without any choice of selection.

When my local production contact couldn't arrange a barber promptly to give my actors a unique bald look, chaos ensued. Flustered by the barber's delayed arrival due to the Sunday rush in his shop, tensions ran high. Despite the setback, when the frustrated cameraman questioned the unacceptable delay, I calmly suggested, 'If it was just a simple shave, I would've handled it with my razor, but we need those signature ponytails on these clean-shaven heads.' Surprisingly, my unconventional solution left him speechless. So there I was, with a snoring cameraman under the cool shade of a tree within minutes. The unexpected turns of events on a seemingly ordinary day of shooting kept us all on our toes.

In the midst of mounting pressure, my patience wore thin as the clock seemed to mock our ambitious shooting schedule. With the first camera position poised from a divine perspective, bathed in meticulous lighting, the daunting task ahead loomed large. The challenge of capturing daylight scenes without the luxury of transforming night into day seemed insurmountable.

Undeterred, I delved into problem-solving mode, knowing that time was a luxury we couldn't afford. Our "dedicated" actors, all so-called seasoned stage performers by my local coordinator, proved to be a beacon of hope. With remarkable speed, they grasped their lines, allowing me to choreograph a seamless movement that brought our vision to life.

As the actors fell into sync with the carefully orchestrated movements and appropriate business, hours slipped away. Exhausted yet determined, we drilled the scene tirelessly until the sun reached its zenith, signalling the call for a well-deserved lunch break.

Amidst the hushed murmurs of the crew settling into a brief respite, a sudden ray of hope emerged with the arrival of the long-awaited barber. With swift precision, he transformed our actors into characters ready for the impending shoot.

Glancing at my watch, the harsh reality of time sank in—it was nearly five in the evening, with sunset fast approaching at six ten. With a silent prayer on my lips, I signalled for action, diving headfirst into the race against time. As the camera rolled, tension hung heavy in the air.

Minutes felt like seconds as the scene unfolded, the magazine's rhythmic churning a metronome to our heartbeat. Miraculously, the first segment was flawlessly captured, a testament to our collective determination. With a quick reload, we plunged back into the fray, chasing the fleeting rays of daylight as if our lives depended on it.

"Cut! And pack up."

As the clock struck twenty past five, a collective sigh of relief enveloped the set as the pivotal scene unfolded flawlessly. A wave of elation swept through the crew, a testament to our perseverance and teamwork.

Months later, as our film graced the screens of the prestigious Pune International Film Festival, renowned filmmaker Dr Jabbar Patel bestowed a rare honour upon us. With discerning eyes, he singled out the meticulously crafted scene, marvelling at its seamless execution and choreographed brilliance.

Reflecting on the gruelling process behind the deceptively smooth final product, I found myself nodding in agreement with Dr Patel's astute observation. "Yes... it was indeed a monumental challenge," I admitted during a group discussion. "It demanded eight arduous hours of dedication and coordination from my exceptional team and talented actors. Without their unwavering support, such a feat would have been out of reach."

In that moment of recognition, amidst accolades and applause, I couldn't help but feel a swell of pride for my cool and calm attitude, which transformed a seemingly insurmountable task into a moment of cinematic magic.

The climax of the film posed yet another formidable challenge, centred around Sane Guruji's impassioned crusade for the entry of Harijan into the temple—an incendiary moment that demanded grandeur and scale to do justice to its historical significance. In reality, the scene unfolded in a dramatic open debate, drawing a staggering crowd of around one lakh fervent followers.

The essence of Sane Guruji's fervour and the monumental gathering became the heart of this pivotal scene, a moment that epitomised his unwavering commitment to social justice. It was clear that capturing this fervent energy on screen was paramount, as omitting or downsizing this spectacle would have diluted the film's impact and compromised its authenticity.

In today's cinematic landscape, the use of VFX could have seamlessly brought this grand spectacle to life. However, back in 2004, with limited resources and virtually no budget for elaborate crowd scenes or special effects, the task of recreating such a monumental event seemed invincible. The sheer magnitude of the challenge underscored the determination and ingenuity required to capture the essence of Sane Guruji's historic confrontation in all its visceral glory.

My decision to tackle the monumental scene on the actual location at Ammalner in northern Maharashtra was a bold and inspired choice, a testament to my dedication to authenticity and respect for Sane Guruji's legacy. The significance of capturing this pivotal moment in a place so closely tied to Sane Guruji's life and teachings would have added a layer of poignancy and depth to the scene, elevating its impact.

Despite the logistical challenges and the producer's assurance of a modest crowd of one to two hundred people, I recognised the irreplaceable value of authenticity over artificial replication. The authenticity of the location and the genuine presence of Sane Guruji's followers lent a certain gravitas and emotional resonance that no amount of visual effects could have replicated.

While the producer may have envisioned a simple workaround with the magic of filmmaking, my insistence on preserving the integrity and spirit of the scene spoke volumes about my commitment to storytelling and honouring Sane Guruji's legacy with the respect and authenticity it deserved. This unwavering dedication to craft and detail was a testimony to my artistic integrity and reverence for the story I wanted to narrate.

As expected, gathering a hundred authentic-looking crowd proved impossible for me, with the new local production person. To my dismay, only a few college students and small kids showed up, expecting to see a famous star, but left disappointed when asked to don old period costumes. Determined not to compromise, I made the bold decision to press on. Changing the schedule, I swiftly pivoted to shooting different scenes, reserving the grand spectacle for our final day.

One night, as I sought solace outside the rest house where we were staying, a chance encounter with an elderly man at the village bus stop altered the course of my thoughts. Gazing at the stars, lost in my thoughts, he approached me and casually inquired, "Seem troubled, any vexations plaguing your mind?" I couldn't help but open up to him about my worries. With a mysterious wisdom in his eyes, he uttered, "Never underestimate Guruji's influence. Plead from your heart, and miracles shall unfold." Intrigued by his cryptic advice, I resolved to explore this uncharted path. The following day, driven by a newfound determination, I penned an impassioned appeal, splashing it across the front page of the local newspaper. And then, as if touched by magic, the extraordinary unfolded before my eyes.

On the day of the shoot, my eyes widened in disbelief as trucks laden with nearby villagers adorned in traditional attire streamed in, each carrying their own tiffin. A sea of three to four thousand souls settled on the sun-baked ground in 38-degree heat, leaving me awestruck. The production team fretted over the logistics of managing such a mammoth crowd. Without hesitation, I stepped onto the dusty earth and prostrated myself, offering heartfelt gratitude to each and every soul. Taking a deep breath, I addressed the vast gathering, spending precious moments bonding with them. I elucidated the scene and their pivotal role, igniting a spark of unity among us all. As the cameras began to roll, the day unfolded like a dream, wrapping up before the sun reached its zenith.

Amidst the throng stood a venerable old gentleman, over ninety years of age, tears glistening in his eyes. With trembling words, he shared a poignant revelation - he had been blessed to witness the original assembly of Sane Guruji at the tender age of six, and now, decades later, he beheld the reincarnation of that momentous day. Touched by his sincerity, I halted his attempt to touch my feet. Humbly, he implored me to partake in the simple meal he had brought. Overwhelmed, I felt my composure waver. The taste and scent of that day's humble Bhakri and the local vegetable he shared with me still linger on my tongue, a potent reminder of the enduring power of human connection and shared memories.

The journey of my career as a filmmaker is woven with moments of countless enriching experiences, each a valuable gem in the mosaic of my life's journey. Reflecting on this intricate weave, I hold a deep-seated belief that one's existence finds true meaning when it is enriched not just by personal victories but by a treasury of wisdom, mistakes, solutions, and lived experiences.

Imagine life as a grand adventure, a quest where we accumulate a diverse array of treasures along the way. These treasures are not jewels to be hoarded in a private vault; rather, they are meant to be shared with others to illuminate their paths and enrich their narratives. Just as a candle loses nothing by lighting another, sharing our wealth of experiences and insights not only benefits those around us but also completes a vital cycle of learning and growth within ourselves.

Let me take you back to 1987, to a remarkable episode that defied all odds through unwavering passion and commitment during my early days in Mumbai's amateur theatre scene. A close friend of mine took the reins as director for a play that I had penned. An enthusiastic group from the naval dockyard was staging this play, a poignant tale inspired by a real-life incident from my childhood in Goa. The play was supposed to be staged in a state-level competition, which was considered the most prestigious. Winning accolades in this experimental venture was akin to a life-and-death situation for the group producing it.

The story unfolded in a remote village grappling with the challenges of modernisation, echoing the heart-wrenching reality. Faced with a dire shortage of drinking water, the villagers approached the government for assistance. In a swift bureaucratic response, a dam was constructed on a nearby river to address their immediate need. Little did they realise that this solution came at a heartbreaking cost - the entire picturesque village was submerged beneath the dam's reservoir, displacing its inhabitants and shattering their ties to their ancestral land.

This poignant saga encapsulated the essence of sacrifice, the struggle for survival, and the bittersweet journey of a community torn from its roots and forced to begin a new in unfamiliar surroundings. When I wrote the play, I ended with one single dialogue: "...And the entire village died down in the dam's reservoir."

My director friend challenged me, saying, "You consider yourself from the film media. How would you have ended the film with the same story?"

"Clearly depicting the village submerged in water."

"So why can't you do it here?"

"On stage?"

"Why not?"

He faced a daunting challenge with no clear path to execute it on stage but harboured unwavering confidence in my abilities to bring it to life. In the technologically limited landscape of 1987, devoid of the aid of Google, my task began with sourcing underwater visuals. After studying numerous pictures from assorted books, I deduced that the key elements of underwater imagery encompassed a hazy ambience, sun rays streaking through from above, and the shimmer of moving water.

I started working on the execution of this spectacle. There was no dearth of manpower. Technical resources like fabricators, carpenters, and tailors were in abundance. Our rehearsals were happening in the naval dockyard premises. One day, I found a couple of dockyard workers rolling a huge plastic transparent sheet in the adjoining warehouse. Normally, some of their machines were transported wrapped in such sheets. My creative mind started ticking. Instantly, the idea struck me that this could be used for moving water. I asked the Commandant officer, who was also an actor in the play, to stitch a transparent plastic curtain of forty feet by thirty-five feet, which was the size of the proscenium opening of the stage. His carpentry team beautifully created a roll-down plastic curtain for us. Ideally, I wanted to test everything in a grand technical rehearsal, but that was not possible for various reasons. All trusted me and my vision for the final result.

As the grand day arrived, the play kicked off with a resounding bang. Applause thundered through the theatre as the curtains drew open, revealing a breathtakingly realistic set. At the heart of the stage stood an imposing banyan tree, its presence commanding attention, surrounded by quaint huts that dotted the perimeter. Dangling branches from above, coupled with the strategically placed lights casting mesmerising sunlight streaks, brought the entire scene to life in a vivid display of artistry and ambience.

While conventional lighting choices typically revolved around white and blue hues to denote day and night transitions, a stroke of creativity sparked within me. For the climactic final scene, I introduced an additional row of green lights, injecting a burst of vibrant colour into the narrative and infusing the stage with an otherworldly allure that captured the audience's imagination and left them spellbound.

The crescendo of excitement surged to its zenith as the play hurtled towards its climactic finale. As the concluding song commenced, a hush fell over the stage, plunging it into darkness. In this veil of obscurity, a plastic curtain descended, swaying gently in the open-air theatre, imbued with a mystical life of its own. A series of lights positioned before the curtain cast a mesmerising shimmer as the stage was bathed in a mystical glow. Above, a cascade of green lights cascaded down like emerald rain while smoke billowed and bubbles danced, orchestrated by fifteen dedicated volunteers. (Silent smoke and bubble machines were not available in those times) In a striking spectacle that defied the limitations of its time, the stage erupted in a symphony of light and ethereal effects, captivating the audience in a spellbinding trance.

The crowd, gripped by the awe-inspiring display before them, remained suspended in sheer astonishment, frozen in their seats for what felt like an eternity. A deafening silence permeated the auditorium, casting a paralysing spell over all present. After a moment that stretched to the brink of time itself, a thunderous applause erupted, breaking the stillness with a surge of fervent approval. Even as the lights dimmed to a velvety blackness and the curtain gracefully descended for the final act, the applause continued, echoing in waves that reverberated throughout the audience. The resounding ovation persisted even as the house lights flickered back on, a proof to the awe-inspiring magic that had unfolded before their very eyes, etching an indelible memory that lingered long after the curtains had closed.

Our play emerged victorious, clinching the first prize, with my efforts recognised and honoured with the award for best lights and stage design. Reflecting back on the journey, I could not envision the play without the breathtaking finale effect that became its defining moment. What started as a daunting challenge transformed into an opportunity through dedication and a relentless hunger for knowledge. Building on this triumph, I later received accolades for stage and light design in a professional production titled 'Double Game', earning a state medal alongside my esteemed mentors who stood as my competitors.

When we generously offer the wealth of our journey to others, we transcend the boundaries of individual accomplishments and forge connections that transcend time and space. Through sharing, we become part of something greater, a collective bundle of shared knowledge and human experience that transcends individual limitations. It is in these moments of imparting wisdom, exchanging stories, and offering guidance that we find a profound sense of fulfilment and purpose.

By letting our experiences flow outward, we create ripples that touch the lives of others, shaping destinies and inspiring new narratives. The act of sharing becomes a evidence to our interconnectedness, a reminder that our stories are not solitary epics but threads in a vast, ever-evolving narrative of humanity.

So, I decided to gather my treasures of wisdom and experience and let their light shine brightly for all to see. Embracing the joy of sharing, I not only enrich the lives of others but also find a deep sense of wholeness and completion within myself.

❖

6

EXPECT THE UNEXPECTED, EVERY DAY

In my nearly four-decade journey through the realm of filmmaking, a singular truth has emerged as the most valuable and profound insight: Expect the Unexpected. Despite meticulous planning, attention to detail, and thorough preparation, there remains an undeniable certainty that the unexpected will inevitably weave its way into the tapestry of our endeavours.

During an extensive tenure spanning nearly a decade, I had the privilege of being an integral part of the country's premier production service company, Stratum Films. Specialising in collaborations with international advertising agencies and production houses, Stratum Films provided a platform for me to engage with some of the industry's finest producers and directors from around the globe. This chapter stands out in my career as one of the most rewarding periods, offering not only valuable insights and knowledge but also significant financial gains.

Undertaking the monumental Tanqueray Gin film project, every dawn heralded a fresh surprise, making each day a saga of its own. Helmed by the acclaimed American ad filmmaker, Tom Kuntz.

Tom Kuntz is an American director and filmmaker best known for his distinctive television commercials and music videos, featuring colourful settings or wildly eccentric characters. He has received several nominations for the title of 'Best Commercial Director of the Year' by the DGA (2007, 2009, 2010, 2013, 2016).

In August 2010, Kuntz's Old Spice "The Man Your Man Could Smell Like" spot won the Emmy for "Commercial of the Year."

Working with him as his First Assistant was a great honour. This cinematic endeavour marked a pivotal moment in my career. Unlike my experiences with Indian directors, collaborating as the chief assistant or first assistant director with a Hollywood luminary revealed a distinct dynamic. In this realm, the first assistant director holds a paramount position, akin to being the linchpin of the set. Tasked with planning, organising, and orchestrating the entire production alongside the director, the first assistant director is the unsung maestro behind the scenes. Their meticulous handiwork begins long before the cameras roll, diligent detailing each scene's execution, working in tandem with the director's assistant to craft a seamless vision on set.

Rodney Mason was brought in as the lead actor. Filled with images of Fred Astaire and the Nicholas Brothers, Rodney could shuffle, hop, boogie, and freestyle with the best. His active imagination carried him through his service as a Marine and brought him to Chicago, where he worked with 2nd City. Then to Los Angeles, where he was recognised with the Olivier Award for his work with Rennie Harris in the hip-hop Shakespearean 'Rome & Jewel'. Rodney has a strong and loyal fan base for his stand-up and one-man shows. He actively developed projects with Tanqueray and Grey Advertising for his persona as "Tony Sinclair." He was also active as a voice-over actor, having worked alongside other major stars for Focus Feature.

This project was a ten-day shoot set against the backdrop of a variety of compelling locations: lush lime gardens, dense jungles, tranquil riverbeds, majestic palaces, and bustling, dusty Indian markets. It was like embarking on a quest for the exclusive Rangpur lime. Most of the locations were shortlisted around Mumbai, Pune, and Jodhpur.

The cast included esteemed actors like Makarand Deshpande, Tom Alter, and Siddharth Jadhav. Siddharth Jadhav was introduced to international advertising by me. Like Atul Parchure, he too acknowledges my efforts to cast him in the project.

Unexpected Day One

The scene was set in a magnificent palace just outside Mumbai. In this pivotal moment, Tony Sinclair and his team arrive at the lavish Palace Hotel. The director had a clear vision: a vintage Land Rover to serve as the key prop, adding an authentic touch of grandeur and elegance to the scene.

My production designer and I had embarked on a relentless quest across Mumbai and Pune, scouring every possible lead before the shoot. We sifted through countless collections and visited numerous vintage car enthusiasts. It felt like searching for a needle in a haystack.

After days of exhaustive searching and overcoming countless obstacles, our perseverance paid off. In Pune, we finally discovered a stunning vintage Land Rover, its timeless charm and impeccably maintained exterior perfect for our needs. The feeling of triumph was palpable.

We secured the car and ensured its safe transport to the palace location, knowing that this iconic vehicle would bring an added layer of historical prestige and visual splendour to Tony Sinclair's grand entrance. As we watched the Land Rover roll into the palace grounds, gleaming under the sunlight, we knew all our efforts had been worth it.

The owner of the vintage Land Rover, proudly driving the car himself from Pune to Mumbai, insisted that only his driver handle it during the shoot. We had no choice but to agree. During the lunch break, one of our main actors struck up a friendly conversation with the owner, and they ended up sitting in the precious Land Rover, discussing its features.

In a casual moment, the owner encouraged the actor to try it out. To everyone's shock, as the actor started the engine and began to manoeuvre, the car suddenly lurched forward and crashed into the palace wall. The right side was badly dented, and the headlight shattered. For a fraction of a second, my heart stopped.

While the incident was technically between the owner and the actor, the Land Rover was our key prop, and we had no choice but to accept responsibility. To salvage the day's shoot, we had to quickly revise our shot division, changing the car's movement from left to right to avoid showing the damaged side.

A special vintage mechanic worked through the night to repair the car. From that moment on, the producer ensured that the actor never went near any of our expensive props again.

Unexpected Day Two

We needed to shoot in the lime fields of a remote village near Pune, called Jejuri. The local farmers were cursing the nature gods due to delayed rains, leaving the crops looking dull and lifeless. To ensure the fields appeared lush and vibrant, we hired water tankers to sprinkle water at regular intervals.

Our art director constructed an impressive, towering gate nearly forty feet high to make the Rangpur lime groves look captivating on screen.

On the day of the shoot, our total crew strength was almost three hundred and fifty people. The convoy of vehicles, including cars, vanity vans, trucks, and tempos from various departments, totalled around one hundred and fifty. It was a monumental effort to bring the scene to life, but the preparation and coordination paid off.

I painstakingly planned every detail for the shoot at Jejuri: holding areas, parking zones, craft and lunch spaces, makeup and wardrobe vans. The international crew required constant internet access, so we even arranged for a special leased line. Every conceivable pro and con were addressed. Our schedule was tight: one day at Jejuri before moving 60 kilometres to the next location. The plan was to wrap by 5:00 pm, allowing vehicles to move on as they completed.

By 4:00 pm, everything was on track. We were elated when the director decided to finish early, granting us an extra half an hour for the company move. But then, as if to mock our hard work, the sky began to darken. Black clouds gathered ominously, and strong winds began to howl.

The director and main actors had already moved to the hotel for the next day's shoot. I stayed behind to oversee the company move, while my assistant and a production man were ready at the new location to guide incoming vehicles and manage logistics.

Without warning, the heavens opened up. A torrential downpour began, almost like a thunderstorm. The farmers rejoiced, blessing us for seemingly bringing the rain they had desperately awaited. But for us, it was catastrophic. The rain pounded down for two relentless hours, turning the ground into a quagmire. Vehicles were hopelessly mired in wet mud, and any attempt to extricate them only made things worse.

"What about tomorrow's shoot?" I asked my production controller, my voice cracking with urgency.

"Give me time to think," he responded, his face tense with concentration.

We battled the elements all night, striving to reverse our predicament. Calls were made to arrange tractors to pull out the trucks and cars, but their weight made it impossible. In a desperate attempt to find a solution, we hired thick wooden planks from Mumbai, constructing a makeshift road.

Hour by gruelling hour, we pulled the vehicles out, inch by painstaking inch. Exhaustion battled with determination as we fought through the night.

By the first light of dawn, the last vehicle finally reached the next location at 8:30 am—just thirty minutes before our international crew was scheduled to arrive at 9:00 am.

The tension and stress had been overwhelming, but we had prevailed. Against all odds, the shoot would go on.

Unexpected Day Three

In the riveting tale of our Tanqueray Gin film production, a cascade of unforeseen events unfolded, transforming our extensively detailed out shoot into an epic saga of resilience and quick thinking. Imagine the bustling chaos of Mumbai's Crawford Market as the backdrop for Tony Sinclair's quest, the air heavy with the promise of impending showers. With the DOP's apprehensions echoing in the background, we braced ourselves for the day's trials, unaware of the tumultuous storm lurking on the horizon.

As the heavens unleashed their fury upon Mumbai, our carefully laid plans dissolved in the rain, forcing us to pivot to Plan B with unwavering speed and determination. The decision to relocate to Jodhpur, Rajasthan, a landscape ripe with authenticity and scorching heat, seemed like a stroke of fate. Tickets were hastily secured, and our ensemble of crew and actors eagerly gathered at the airport, ready to embark on a journey fraught with uncertainty.

The change in aircraft from a Boeing 737 to an ATR aircraft marked the beginning of our uphill battle, as weight restrictions held our critical equipment captive in Mumbai. The airline's proposed multi-leg journey for our cargo sent shivers down our spines, heralding a logistical nightmare in the making.

Amid mounting tension and a foreboding prophecy from a local informant in Jodhpur, our resolve was tested to the fullest. With our gear stranded in Jaipur due to a transport strike, our plans hung in the balance. Seizing control of the situation, we orchestrated a daring plan to convert a private bus into a cargo carrier by stripping it bare, a bold move born out of sheer necessity and determination.

As the sun peeked over the horizon in Jodhpur, our makeshift cargo bus rumbled into view, a symbol of our unwavering spirit and unyielding resolve in the face of adversity. The incredulous amazement of the international crew at our unconventional solution only added to the grandeur of our cinematic journey through the unpredictable terrain of filmmaking. Our expedition had tested our mettle, but ultimately, it was a testament to our unwavering commitment to craft and camaraderie in the face of the unexpected.

Amidst the whirlwind of unexpected challenges that punctuated our frenzied ten-day shooting schedule, a particularly peculiar conundrum emerged during a crucial scene featuring Tony Sinclair as an aborigine relishing barbecued meat on a wooden skewer in the heart of the jungle. A sudden revelation from the director's assistant sent shockwaves through our meticulously laid plans - Rodney Meson, in character, staunchly refused to consume any real meat. The race against time had begun to find a vegetarian alternative that not only looked convincingly like barbecued meat but was also palatable to our finicky actor.

As panic threatened to tighten its grip around us, brainstorming sessions yielded no viable solutions in our remote village shooting locale. Just when all hope seemed lost, a flash of inspiration struck me. Recalling a humble pakoda (savoury fritter of onion and gram flour) vendor I had encountered during our scouting mission, I swiftly sprang into action. Instructing my resourceful production team to procure a supply of piping hot onion pakodas from the local vendor, I emphasised the need for them to resemble barbecued meat and be presented in a suitable container from our catering department.

In just ten minutes, the fragrant aroma of the crispy pakoras filled the air, their appearance uncannily resembling the desired barbecued meat, slightly charred to perfection as per my directive. Rodney's initial scepticism melted away as he tentatively sampled the unconventional substitute. A wave of delight washed over him as he relished the unexpected treat, bestowing upon it a newfound appreciation. By the scene's conclusion, Rodney had transcended from a dubious observer to a fervent devotee of the delectable Indian "Kanda Bhajji," forever etching a savoury memory amidst the whirlwind of our unpredictable filmmaking odyssey.

By now, it should be clear that sharp and dynamic production control is crucial to running a successful film unit. We were fortunate to have a production controller like Manish Trehan with us during the Tanqueray shoot. His decision-making ability was outstanding, and he was supported by Avinash Shankar, an equally competent and accommodating producer.

In Hindu belief, it is often said that when you meet someone in life, it is destined or preordained by destiny. This concept aligns with the idea of fate, karma, and the interconnected nature of relationships in Hindu philosophy. They say that anyone who comes into your life either makes you or breaks you but teaches you a lesson for life. Avinash Chowgule taught me what not to do, and Avinash Shankar taught me what to do. Avinash Chowgule, a talented individual with immense potential, tragically passed away at a very young age. He took his own life by jumping from the eighth floor of his residence. The reasons behind this heartbreaking act remain unknown, but the loss left a deep void in the hearts of those who knew him.

After a few days, my former boss and the President of the advertising agency reached out to me, inviting me to his residence in Pedder Road. Coincidentally, I was shooting at a studio in Pedder Road at the time. As I stood before him, he greeted me with unexpected respect and honour, a gesture that caught me off guard. It was during our conversation that he shed light on the past, acknowledging that our parting had been a hasty decision. He admitted that after working on a couple of projects with the individual in question, it became evident that I was not to blame. With a sense of closure, he remarked, "Things unfold in their own time." He extended his well wishes for my future endeavours. This encounter served as a poignant reminder that sometimes, those who once accused us may eventually realise their misjudgements. While their recognition may provide some solace, the repercussions of past accusations linger, underscoring the irrevocable impact such misunderstandings can have. I was profoundly affected by his untimely demise and grieved for him and his family. It's a stark reminder of the hidden struggles people may face, often unnoticed by those around them. This tragic event made me reflect on the importance of mental health and the need to support one another through difficult times.

As I continued with my work, I carried the memory of Avinash Chowgule with me, a reminder of the fragility of life and the silent battles many endure. His story is evidence to the importance of compassion and understanding, both in our professional and personal lives.

Executive Producer Avinash Shankar has played a pivotal role in shaping my journey towards success. His unwavering support and numerous opportunities have been instrumental in my growth. As both First Assistant Director and producer, he offered me roles that not only challenged me but also allowed me to flourish with grace and dignity. Words cannot express the depth of my gratitude for his belief in me and his willingness to invest in my potential. I will always hold an immense appreciation for Avinash Shankar and his invaluable contributions to my career, and I will carry this gratitude with me throughout my life.

I was associated with Avinash Shankar for almost fifteen years. "In my experience, I have come to understand how working with a single company for an extended period can sometimes impede personal growth by limiting exposure to the outside world. It's true that long tenures within a company can provide a sense of stability and security, but they can also create a barrier to individual development in several ways.

Continuously working with one company for an extended period can potentially hinder individual growth by restricting exposure to diverse experiences and perspectives from the outside world. While long tenures within a single company can offer stability, familiarity, and a sense of security, there are several ways in which this may limit personal development:

Limited Exposure: Remaining within the same company may limit exposure to new ideas, technologies, and methodologies prevalent in other organisations. This lack of exposure can inhibit the growth of one's skill set and knowledge base.

Comfort Zone: Over time, employees may become accustomed to the routines, culture, and expectations of their current workplace, leading to a sense of complacency. Stepping out of this comfort zone and engaging with different work environments can foster adaptability, creativity, and resilience.

Networking Opportunities: Working in a single company for an extended period may limit opportunities to build a diverse professional network. Interacting with individuals from various backgrounds and industries can provide valuable insights, foster collaborations, and open doors to new opportunities.

Stagnation: Without exposure to new challenges, perspectives, and ways of working, employees run the risk of stagnation in their professional development. Continuous learning and growth often stem from encountering fresh challenges and pushing boundaries beyond familiar territories.

Adaptability and Innovation: The ability to adapt to changing environments and innovate is crucial in today's dynamic workforce. Spending an extended period in one company may restrict exposure to new trends, technologies, and practices prevalent in other industries.

Personal Development: Engaging with diverse experiences and environments can contribute significantly to personal growth, expanding one's horizons, enhancing problem-solving skills, and fostering a broader perspective.

In summary, while long tenures in a single company can offer stability and deep institutional knowledge, it's essential to seek opportunities for growth, learning, and exposure to diverse experiences outside one's immediate work environment or comfort zone to foster continuous personal and professional development.

Embracing the unexpected and meeting it head-on has been a profound lesson learned through my enduring association with Avinash Shankar. Since 2009 to this day, I have had the privilege of being a part of Avinash Shankar's esteemed production houses, Stratum Films and Blank Slate Ad Com Pvt. Ltd. His unwavering support has opened doors to collaborations with some of the world's most talented creative minds like Tarsem, David Deneen, and various other luminaries. My professional journey has been profoundly enriched through his projects, shaping a CV adorned with remarkable experiences and accomplishments.

The extravagant world travels in business and first-class flights, the luxurious stays in five-star hotels - all bear witness to Avinash's gracious approach in caring for his associates. Over the span of fifteen years, our partnership has blossomed and flourished, with many even mistaking me for his partner due to our close bond. Yet, this familiarity occasionally posed challenges when exploring opportunities with other producers. The lingering question, "Why seek work elsewhere when you are associated with the country's finest producer?" echoed in my pursuit of new ventures. My narrative is incomplete without acknowledging the pivotal role of Stratum, Blank Slate, and Avinash Shankar in shaping my professional odyssey.

At this point, I am reminded of one of my feature film projects during my most challenging days. In 1987, I worked as the Chief Assistant Director with Sukhwant Dhadda on a film titled "Siyasat," which featured a star-studded cast including Kumar Gaurav, Shakti Kapoor, Kimi Katkar, Deepa Sahi, Kulbhushan Kharbanda, and Gulshan Grover, among others. The producer, Shashi Ranjan, also portrayed one of the lead characters.

We had meticulously planned a long outdoor schedule to shoot the climax and several important scenes involving this esteemed cast. Our producer, Shashi Ranjan, hailed from Bhiwani, Haryana, in northern India, and decided to shoot these scenes there, leveraging his extensive contacts and influence in the region.

The shoot was set, and all actors, the director, the producer, and the Director of Photography (DOP) were to depart a day later by flight. The rest of the crew was supposed to travel by train, a journey lasting nearly twenty hours.

On the day of departure, about forty of us gathered at the bustling Central Station, excitement mingling with the usual chaos of train travel. As we assembled with our luggage, the air buzzed with anticipation. However, an unsettling undercurrent ran through the group as we repeatedly asked the production manager for our confirmed tickets. His evasive responses raised our suspicions.

Whispers and questioning glances spread among us. "Where are the tickets?" someone asked, pressing the production person who seemed to dodge direct eye contact. The murmur of concern grew louder, and our patience began to wane.

Our doubt aggravated – did we actually have reservations for this crucial journey? Why the avoidance? Was something amiss? I asked him a straight question. I could see the unease mirrored in his eyes. The tension was palpable, hanging in the air like a brewing storm.

It was then that the realisation hit us. We actually had no reserved seats. The clock was ticking, the train's departure was imminent, and our vital journey was hanging precariously in the balance. We were all asked to push ourselves in the unreserved compartment, which was already oozing out with people.

At one point, the idea of quitting crossed my mind, but as a struggler in the field, I was left with no choice. We were all desperate, and somehow, we managed to push ourselves into the crowded compartment. I barely found a spot to stand as the train departed sharply at 9:00 pm.

The journey was gruelling. From the moment the train left the station until it reached Sawai Madhopur at around 6:00 am, I was on my feet, standing for almost nine relentless hours. Each moment was a test of endurance as I grappled with the constant jostling and rocking of the moving train, performing all sorts of balancing acts to avoid collapsing from sheer exhaustion.

I felt every second stretch into an eternity. My legs screamed in protest, and my body ached from the strain. I was an island of fatigue amid a sea of restless passengers. Just when I thought I could bear no more, a fellow passenger who had observed my plight for hours took pity on me. With a compassionate glance, he shifted just enough to allow me to rest one side on the seat, offering me the smallest yet most precious relief.

At that moment, his small gesture felt like salvation, a brief respite from an otherwise unyielding ordeal. Even in such dire straits, the human spirit shone through in the smallest acts of kindness, giving me the strength to push forward.

At that moment, I made a firm resolution: no matter what happens, I would not continue my struggle in this manner. If it came to it, I would quit the industry and become a vegetable vendor rather than compromise my dignity and endure such hardship. This was my turning point—a self-assessment that solidified my commitment to preserving my self-respect, above all else.

When we finally reached Bhiwani, I expressed my anger and concerns to both the director and the producer. I adamantly refused to shoot the next day, demanding a full day to acclimatise to the situation. Most of the crew members stood by me, as they were all hired on a per-day remuneration and were more than happy to receive a day's pay while resting in the guesthouse.

On this rest day, I encountered a very intriguing character: Neem Singh Beniwal. Standing nearly six feet tall and always dressed in a white kurta and pyjama, he carried a revolver tucked into his waistband. He was perpetually surrounded by a small entourage of five or six people, two of whom were armed with. 303 rifles.

He approached me directly, asking with a piercing gaze, "Why aren't you shooting today?" At first, I felt a surge of fear, almost paralysed by his imposing aura and the armed men surrounding him. Despite my trepidation, I took a deep breath and calmly explained the situation. I recounted the gruelling journey, the lack of consideration for the crew's well-being, and how it all reached a breaking point for me. My voice trembled as I conveyed the exhaustion and the need for a day of rest.

As I spoke, I noticed a change in his expression. The hard lines of his face softened, and to my astonishment, he pulled me into a bear hug. "I like people like you," he said, his voice resonating with warmth and respect, "who are reasonable and protect their self-esteem."

He further added, "Brother! You are my guest here in Bhiwani. Shashi sir told me to check with you when you will start shooting. Don't misunderstand me. I will see to it that you will not have any more problems. Just ask anyone around for Beniwal Bhai, and I will be there at your disposal. Do you drink? I mean English liquor?"

Before I could say anything, he asked one of his men to get some of the best English liquor. His man very politely said, "Wine shops are closed at this hour. It's difficult to get anything."

"Break the lock of Lallan's wine shop and get it now."

All were stunned by this commanding order. No one had the courage to say anything further. Understanding the situation, Beniwal Bhai added more -

"Buy him a new lock tomorrow, first thing in the morning."

In that moment, the fear dissolved, replaced by a sense of validation and unexpected camaraderie. Neem Singh Beniwal's approval and support were a dramatic twist I hadn't anticipated, turning a day of frustration into a moment of empowerment.

Neem Singh Beniwal was truly a dynamic personality. Without his presence and influence, it would have been nearly impossible for us to shoot in a place where even a six-year-old child exhibited full arrogance and defiance.

During one of the preparations, I casually asked a young boy to step back a little, fearing he might wander into the frame. He shot back with a fiery gaze, "Hamari zameen hai, hum kyun piche hatein? Aap hi piche hato!" (This is our land, why should we step back? You step back!)

This defiant attitude from such a young child encapsulated the bold and unyielding spirit of the region. In that moment, the necessity of Beniwal's support was starkly clear. He commanded respect and authority in a land where unwavering pride ran deep, even in the hearts of the young. It was his dynamic leadership that created a bridge between us and this fiercely independent community, making the impossible possible.

We were faced with the challenge of shooting a pivotal scene – a friend's parting moment – at a railway station, without official permission from the government authorities. However, our ever-accommodating director said that we could carry on regardless of the location. In a surprising turn of events, Neem Singh, who had always been a looming presence by our side, erupted with indignation. "How can someone dare object when I am here," he declared.

Turning to me, he said, "Plan your shoot for the Bhiwani Junction station. I'll speak to the station master." In that moment, with Neem Singh's unwavering confidence and authority, none of us had any choice but to simply nod in agreement, knowing that where he led, obstacles crumbled.

The next day, our crew arrived at the Bhiwani Junction location to a surprising sight—the station master, impeccably dressed in his uniform, stood ready to greet us. He reassured us, saying that Beniwal ji had briefed him and we needn't worry about a thing. Turning to the director, he inquired, "I hope this uniform meets your requirements."

The director glanced at me, seeking reassurance. I calmly responded, "I've already spoken to Beniwal ji. Let's capture one shot of the station master waving a green flag."

As luck would have it, an express train was scheduled to pass through Bhiwani Junction in the next fifteen minutes. The director expressed concern, noting that it would be futile if it were merely a through train.

In a dramatic intervention, Beniwal stepped forward, his tone firm and authoritative. "Do not worry, Sir. We will stop the train. You get your lighting ready," he declared, his words imbued with a confidence that brooked no dissent.

Beniwal's assurance transformed the atmosphere, infusing the moment with a sense of urgency and determination. With his command, the seemingly impossible task now seemed within our reach.

"Get ready! Start action! The train is coming!" Beniwal shouted at the top of his lungs. In an instant, everyone moved into action. Four or five massive HMI lights blazed on, their intense beams piercing the air. Almost as if blinded by the sudden flash of light, the express train came to an abrupt halt midway through the station.

Without missing a beat, Beniwal sprinted towards the locomotive, his voice echoing with authority. "Why did you stop here? Don't you understand we are shooting?" he bellowed at the bewildered loco driver, who had never experienced such an intrusion in his life.

The driver, confused and intimidated, listened as Beniwal commanded him to reverse the train and then approach the station again at full speed, stopping precisely at his mark. We stood in stunned silence, not daring to interfere with Beniwal's orders. His formidable presence seemed to bend reality to his will.

Miraculously, the locomotive driver complied, reversing the train and then powering forward once more, stopping perfectly on Beniwal's mark.

As soon as it halted, we sprang into action, efficiently capturing the pivotal scene. The passengers on the express train remained blissfully unaware of the cinematic drama unfolding around them. Before they could register what was happening, our scene was complete, the guard blew his whistle, and the train resumed its journey.

The whirlwind of events felt like a surreal nightmare, leaving us breathless and incredulous. Amidst the chaos, I suddenly remembered our arrangement with the station master. We quickly took his special shot, adroitly waving the green flag—but this time, without the train.

Afterwards, we found a moment of respite in his cabin, where we were greeted with hot, fresh samosas. It was a small but gratifying reward after a day filled with unimaginable drama and unprecedented challenges. The entire experience left an indelible mark, showcasing the extraordinary powers of Neem Singh Beniwal and the unpredictable magic of filmmaking.

During a situation when our special effects team was running low on gunpowder typically used for small blasting effects, I suggested reaching out to Beniwal Bhai for assistance. When our team member contacted Beniwal Bhai, he simply chuckled and referred to the issue as a minor one. Speaking to his associates in their local dialect, Beniwal Bhai's men swiftly arrived with fifty homemade explosives they called 'Desi Grenades.' With ease, he advised us to open up the grenades to retrieve at least five kilograms of gunpowder.

On another occasion, we were scheduled to shoot a curfew scene on a market street, aiming for an eerie, completely empty street with only a few police officers loitering around. Yet, when we arrived at the location, we were met by a sea of spectators lining the street and crowding the balconies, their curious eyes fixed on us. The daunting task of clearing this enormous crowd seemed impossible, and once again, we knew only Beniwal could provide a solution. Half-jokingly, we thought that a couple of shots fired from his revolver might scatter them.

When Beniwal arrived with his entourage, I approached him casually. "We need the street completely empty. It's a crucial curfew scene."

Beniwal paused for a moment, his face contemplating the challenge. He asked one of his men, "What day is it?"

"Sunday," came the reply, the worst day for such a task.

In his characteristically calm yet authoritative tone, Beniwal responded, "Give me until 10 am. I'll clear the street for you for half an hour. Can you shoot within that timeframe?"

Without hesitation, we responded, "Of course!"

As the clock ticked closer to ten AM, we waited with bated breath to witness the magic of Neem Singh Beniwal. Precisely at 10 am, the familiar title music of the immensely popular "Ramayan" TV serial began to play from every direction. Within minutes, the transformation was miraculous. The bustling street emptied as people vanished inside, drawn to their TV sets to catch the episode. The entire market street was deserted, achieving the curfew effect we desperately needed.

"Ramayan" was so beloved, especially in small towns and villages, that its broadcast was almost sacred. The deserted street stood as a testament to its influence.

We quickly shot our scene, capturing the perfect depiction of a curfew. In a mix of relief and awe, we silently thanked Lord Rama for his blessings, marvelling at the high-voltage drama orchestrated by Beniwal and the cultural phenomenon of "Ramayan."

In conclusion, the profound mantra of "expecting the unexpected" has unfolded as a guiding principle in my journey, underpinned by resilience, adaptability, and a steadfast commitment to navigating the twists and turns of fate. Through the valuable lessons gleaned from facing unforeseen challenges head-on, I have emerged fortified with wisdom, humility, and a profound appreciation for the intricacy of life's uncertainties. Embracing the unexpected with an open heart and a determined spirit, I stand poised to embark on the next chapter 'Dream big but dream for living' of my story, fortified by the strength found in the uncharted territories of the unknown.

❖

7

DREAM BIG, DREAM FOR LIVING

Filmmakers are no ordinary individuals; they breathe life into their dreams for others to witness on screen. Regardless of a film's budget, obstacles, or setbacks, a great filmmaker crafts stories that enthral and move audiences emotionally. These qualities aren't innate but cultivated over time. Each person is born with unique strengths and weaknesses, and wisdom lies in recognising and nurturing these traits.

Do I possess the hallmarks of a great filmmaker? Where do my weaknesses lie? Where do my strengths shine? How can I improve and grow? Strengthening weaknesses and amplifying strengths is a continuous journey we can all embark on for success. Adaptation and growth are vital for staying ahead of the competition.

My cinematic knowledge stems solely from hands-on experience; it took years to grasp these nuances. Today's generation is fortunate to have access to esteemed film schools and institutions, and YouTube channels by experienced filmmakers, offering a wealth of knowledge to aspirants at a young age.

In the peaceful tranquillity of our modest home in a quiet Goan town, my meeting with Shantaram Joshi proved to be the crucial turning point that sparked my passion for filmmaking. His talent for narrating a captivating and complete film story, mesmerising the audience for nearly two hours, was truly remarkable. Alongside his storytelling prowess, his subtle yet profound message urging us to "Dream big, but dream for living" echoed throughout my entire career as a guiding principle.

When I asked him in one lonely moment, "How can you remember so many films with such details?" Shantaram, with his soulful gaze, bearing the weight of countless untold stories, in a moment of candid vulnerability, unveiled the path of his past to me.

"I once harboured dreams of gracing the silver screens of the Marathi film industry," his voice resonated with echoes of a bygone era, carrying the weight of unspoken struggles. "Born into poverty, my parents toiled as labourers in our modest village, their dreams as fragile as whispers in the wind. Fate led me to the corridors of Jayaprabha Studio in Kolhapur, where I became a mere sweeper, a silent spectator to the grand performances of cinematic legends."

Glimpses of yesteryears flickered in his eyes as he uttered names that once adorned the silver screen like constellations in the night sky— Chandrakant Suryakant, Asha Kale, Lalita Powar, each a luminary in their own right. "As destiny wove its intricate threads, the elusive gates of the cinematic realm remained closed to me. But in the shadows of unfulfilled aspirations, I unearthed a treasure within myself—an unparalleled gift of recollection."

"In the hallowed confines of the studio, I immersed myself in the world of cinema, watching films with an insatiable hunger for the stories they held. Every frame, every dialogue, every melody became etched in my memory," his words carried the weight of years spent in silent dedication. "Even when sight eluded me, I turned to the melodies of unseen narratives, listening to the symphony of tales unfolding sitting behind the silver screen."

It was amidst the echoes of cinematic splendour that Shantaram found his calling, his path diverging from the spotlight to the shadows, yet leading him to a realm where his gift of remembrance bloomed into a livelihood. "This path chose me as its disciple, offering sustenance and solace in the gentle embrace of storytelling. In the labyrinth of forgotten dreams, I found contentment, and in the echoes of cinematic glory, I discovered a legacy of my own. This, my dear friend, is the tale of how I found my voice amidst the whispers of the silver screen."

This impact at an early age changed my outlook completely. I strongly decided that I should also narrate stories and make money. I even started it with my friends. My privilege of watching movies started transcending as narration with my friends.

The profound impact of those transformative days seeped into the very essence of my being, reshaping my perspective on the world and kindling a fierce determination within me. Witnessing Shantaram's spellbinding performances ignited a fire within my soul, propelling me towards a singular conviction—I too would narrate stories and craft my path to prosperity through the magic of storytelling.

Drawing from the privilege of my cinematic experiences, I embarked on a new journey with fervour, transforming movie-watching sessions with friends into vibrant storytelling sessions. The narratives that once unfolded on celluloid now found resonance in the animated tales I wove for my companions, each anecdote a stepping stone towards a future where my voice would resonate with the power of storytelling.

A revelation unfolded to me. Amidst the realms of reality and imagination colliding, a pact was silently sealed, binding me to a destiny intertwined with the magic of storytelling and the allure of the silver screen. My path was forever altered, leading me down the winding road of cinematic dreams and infinite possibilities.

For a filmmaker, dreaming grandiose dreams comes naturally; it's an inherent part of our creative DNA. However, the true essence of success lies not just in dreaming big but in dreaming for sustenance, for livelihood. The delicate balance between aspiring for greatness and anchoring those dreams in the realm of practicality is where many filmmakers stumble.

In the annals of reminiscences, a singular figure emerged from the sepia-toned memories of my past—Ravi Hirlekar. Our paths intertwined within the hallowed embrace of an amateur theatre group named "Maitra," a sanctuary where dreams took flight amidst the murmurs of whispered aspirations.

Ravi, born of humble origins in a lower middle-class household, ignited fires of ambition that illuminated the very fabric of our shared dreams. His spirit, a tempestuous fusion of grit and grandiosity, soared to heights that even the heavens dared not fathom. Amidst the dusty streets of Mumbai, where ambitions towered like skyscrapers, Ravi stood as a beacon of audacity and perseverance.

With defiant resolve, he clashed against the confines of his reality, a reality where dreams were but fragile tendrils grasping towards the unattainable. In a household where, meagre earnings were stitched together with threads of sacrifice and toil. Ravi's father, a retired postman, trod the sunlit paths, peddling candies and toffees with unwavering dedication. The paltry sum earned through his labours, a mere two hundred to three hundred rupees a day, wove the tapestry of survival for their family.

Yet amidst this ceaseless toil and humble existence, Ravi yearned for the stars, his eyes fixed on a distant horizon. The dream that eclipsed all others—the dream to tread the revered halls of J.J. School of Art— loomed as an insurmountable peak, a summit beyond the reach of his family's modest means. His father's weary form, weathered by years of tireless labour, cast a long shadow of purpose and sacrifice over their lives, his pension interwoven with the humble earnings from candy sales in a poignant dance of survival.

In this delicate balance of dreams and duty, Ravi's younger sister, a beacon of promise amidst the unforgiving currents of reality, pursued her studies with unwavering dedication. Her final year of B'Com stood as a harbinger of hope and possibility for their proud yet unassuming parents. In the maelstrom of adversity and aspiration, Ravi stood as a testament to the resilience of the human spirit, a phoenix rising from the embers of circumstance. His dreams echoed through the corridors of time as a poignant melody of fortitude and fervour.

Ravi was different. Always lost in a creative sphere of his own. Ravi was very much influenced by Remo Fernandes. He did everything in bits and pieces. When asked, "What do you want to do in life?" Ravi's favourite answer was, "I want to enjoy life to the fullest."

In the kaleidoscope of opportunities, we extended to Ravi, a mosaic of potential futures awaiting him. Yet his spirit danced to a different melody—one untethered by the shackles of traditional trajectories. When I proffered a golden chance in the realms of advertising, a foothold in the enchanting world of filmmaking as my assistant, his response lingered in the hallowed echoes of his unwavering spirit.

"I refuse to engulf myself in the nine-to-six vicious circle," his words, a poignant declaration of independence, rang with a clarity born of unyielding resolve. Ravi, a maverick spirit, found solace not in the structured confines of corporate corridors but in the unfettered realms of creativity and wit, where his talents as a raconteur and entertainer shone like beacons in the night.

Ravi's whimsy and wit carved a niche that none could replicate. His jests, anecdotes, and magnetic presence wove a spell of levity and laughter. He shared moments that enriched our lives and endeared him to our hearts. As guardians of his dreams, we enveloped him in a blanket of understanding and care, knowing that his path, though unconventional, bore the seeds of brilliance and possibility.

Ravi stood as a visionary ahead of his time, a luminary weaving threads of innovation and creativity in a landscape often bound by convention. In the year 1984, long before the resonant beats of rap songs touched the shores of Mumbai in 2012, his compositions soared above the zeitgeist, a testament to his pioneering spirit and artistic boldness.

As his words unfurled in the rhythmic cadence of rap, the echoes of his songs reverberated through the corridors of our shared experiences, each verse a testament to his innate talent and audacity. The melodies he crafted, and the verses he penned, bore the imprints of a genius untamed, an artist unbound by the constraints of time or tradition. With each rhyme and rhythm, Ravi painted a vivid picture of lyrical prowess that transcended the boundaries of the ordinary.

In the embrace of his music, we found solace and exhilaration, an otherworldly journey propelled by the raw energy and unbridled creativity that defined Ravi's artistry. His songs, a symphony of the unconventional and the avant-garde, resonated with a vibrancy that left us yearning for more, a proof to the transformative power of his vision.

In the annals of our collective memory, we marvelled at the brilliance that was Ravi, imagining a world where his talents bloomed on a global stage. His mastery of rap and hip-hop, a genre then unknown to our shores, left us pondering what might have been if he had been born in foreign lands—to herald in a new era of music, to carve his name among the pioneers of rap culture, and to weave his legacy into the very fabric of artistic innovation.

In the intricate journey of his existence, tragedy unfurled its cruel design around Ravi, entangling him in a labyrinth of torment and despair. The burdens of the world cascaded upon his shoulders, as the weight of caring for his beloved sister fell solely upon him, following the departure of his ailing parents. Their final journey completed, they had weathered life's storms until the burden grew beyond their mortal grasp, leaving a void in their wake.

Grief intermingled with the shadows of a troubled mind, casting a pall of mental anguish upon his sister, her spirit adrift in the tempest of loss and upheaval. In the forge of adversity, Ravi stood as a steadfast guardian, a pillar of unyielding devotion amidst the tumultuous waves of fate. Shouldering the weight of responsibility with grace and fortitude, he navigated the ebb and flow of life's unyielding currents, a stalwart presence in the face of relentless trials.

As the shadows lengthened over his path, Ravi toiled tirelessly, his artistry dimmed by the harsh glare of exploitation and unfulfilled promises. The world heaved its demands upon him, extracting his talents with callous disregard, yet he bore his burdens with a resilience that belied the cracks in his armour. Amidst the cacophony of betrayals and broken dreams, his smile remained a beacon of light, a evidence to the indomitable spirit that burned within him.

And then, as if fate itself conspired to add another layer of tragedy to his tale, the news descended like a shroud of darkness. Ravi, our dear friend, had departed this realm for the heavenly abode, a month slipping by unnoticed as his body lay in solitary repose. His once-vibrant presence faded into the silence of an unattended room, his sister lost in the labyrinth of her own mind, a silent witness to the solitude that engulfed them.

Four days passed, each heartbeat a dirge of abandonment as his spirit hovered on the cusp of eternity. It was only when the world outside stirred with murmurs of disquiet that the door to his haven was breached, revealing a scene of heart-wrenching desolation. Kind neighbours, moved by a sense of duty and compassion, bridged the chasm of neglect, bestowing upon Ravi the final rites that whispered of closure and peace.

As the final threads of his story wove into the fabric of memory, I bowed my head in silent prayer, beseeching the Almighty to cradle Ravi's soul in a gentle embrace, granting him the solace and rest that eluded him in life. May his spirit soar on wings of eternal light, unshackled from the burdens that weighed him down, finding respite in the celestial expanse where sorrows are but whispers in the wind, and peace reigns eternal.

Navigating the expanse between lofty aspirations and pragmatic goals is a formidable task—one that tests the resilience and foresight of every storyteller. It's at this pivotal juncture that the path to success diverges for many, where some lose sight of the need for sustainability amidst their soaring dreams. Mastering this art of harmonising ambition with practicality is the true hallmark of a filmmaker destined for greatness.

It is effortless to immerse oneself in the realm of dreams, but translating those dreams into reality demands meticulous consideration of all facets: from personal capacity and available resources to the critical element of deadlines. If all efforts to manifest your celluloid dream falter, it is wise to pause, recalibrate, and redirect your focus towards alternate aspirations. Remember, the journey from envisioning a dream to seeing it materialise is a dynamic interplay of timing and preparation. By nurturing flexibility and resilience, one can gracefully shelve a dream for the moment with the unwavering faith that the opportune moment will inevitably dawn when circumstances align harmoniously to bring your dream project to fruition.

In the hazy dance between dreams and reality, I learned a harsh lesson— one that etched its tale into the recesses of my being. Temptation wore the guise of an executive producer, luring me with promises of transforming my enigmatic vision into a televised odyssey. The seed of this venture had sprouted in the depths of an obscure, mysterious incident during my days as an assistant director on a Marathi serial, a tale that begged to be narrated in the world of storytelling.

The television industry in India during that time worked on a completely different mindset. Especially before the invasion of OTT platforms, the executive producer of the channel was considered the supreme authority. No questions asked, and 'do as they say' was the basic principle of success. Their way of functioning was totally based on TRP ratings. I am not blaming them entirely as it was true that a different generation of television viewers was emerging rapidly. Watching a particular serial at a specific time was akin to an addiction. This trend still continues but is declining with the introduction of OTT channels.

I recall a situation where one of my friends left his home and went into exile for a unique reason. He resided with his mother and held a position at a well-known automobile company. His mother had a strong addiction to prime-time soap operas. Upon his return from work, he consistently discovered his mother engrossed in the television, with the volume set to maximum. The serials of that era presented endless narratives lacking logic and realism, filled with expected twists and turns. This trend drove serious and authentic filmmakers to the brink of frustration.

I decided to enter the world of television in my pursuit of 'dream big and dream for living.' I came from a background of a limited series with a definite beginning and end. That's what I had learned in my entire career. The duration of the serial should depend on the content of the story. Sagas like Ramayan and Mahabharat need a considerably long duration as the content spans generations with plots and subplots. The sheer size of characters in these sagas alone is so vast that introducing them would require several episodes. Nevertheless, even they reach a definite conclusion.

But these so-called modern soap operas were like a flowing river, moving in the direction of a slope with a gravitational pull of the so-called television rating point or target rating point (TRP). I also came from a solid ten-year background in advertising, where every detail is planned well in advance with meticulous planning, precision, and perfection.

I had just left an advertising agency with good financial stability and was focused on my goal of becoming a filmmaker. At this juncture, I met a lady who was an executive producer at a highly respected television channel. She casually suggested, "Why don't you create something for television?" I then narrated my personal encounter with an obscure, enigmatic incident that I had experienced while working as an assistant director in a mysterious village. The lady executive, clearly impressed, insisted that I turn my story into a television serial for their channel. Although hesitant, I agreed to discuss the proposal with some friends in the television industry before deciding. However, she pushed me to accept a proposal approval letter, marking the inception of my own production house,

ESBE Soundvision. It was her idea to name it SB Soundvision, with SB representing Sandeep and Bhagyashree. Everything unfolded so quickly that I had little time to reflect. Furthermore, my close friends questioned, "Why hesitate? Everything is falling into your lap effortlessly."

Propelled by the fervour of the lady executive producer's excitement, I dove headfirst into crafting a proposal that pulsated with the heartbeat of my animated story. Encouragement echoed around me, painting this opportunity as a once-in-a-lifetime venture that every filmmaker yearns for. Blinded by overconfidence and entranced by the allure of my dream project, I leapt into the abyss of production, my mind ensnared by the vision dancing in my head.

The groundwork was meticulous, the locations handpicked, the cast carefully chosen—every detail planned without pausing to consider the exigencies of the television serial. My biggest mistake was treating this small-screen venture as a mega big-screen saga. Managing dates, accommodations, travel, and other logistics was like a nightmare. My wife Bhagyashree, as the producer, was finding it very hard to strike a balance between incoming and outgoing resources. Amidst the chorus of advice from all corners, I was repeatedly told, "In the television industry, you sow before you reap. At first, invest without expecting immediate returns from the channel, and in due time, watch the profits march towards you like loyal soldiers."

Upon completion of the pilot episode, I eagerly presented it to the channel. The lady executive lauded it as nothing short of extraordinary. At the same time, she suggested two small changes: change this actor and change this location. How can someone justify these changes as small changes just because she didn't like them? I said, "These minor adjustments will have significant cost implications for me. The selection of this actor and specific location was a intentional choice, made after careful deliberation and intense brainstorming with my creative team." I was somewhat irritated but made a conscious effort to conceal it on my face.

"Kashyap, sir! This is how the industry works. You seem new to this industry. I request you to maintain the protocol," her assistant said in a very impudent manner. On top of this, the lady executive supported him by nodding her head. Her swollen mouth, filled with a wad of chewing tobacco, prevented her from speaking.

Bhagyashree, my wife and the producer, pulled out of the meeting to avoid further conflict and said, "This time let's do what she is saying as we've invested a lot in this episode."

"What if she continues her attitude?" I was very realistic and convinced.

"Let's take a chance. We will mention to her that it will not be possible to change anything after the approval of the final shooting script and proceed from their side." Before I could counter her, Bhagyashree said, "I know that this time also we had followed the same procedure, but she is demanding changes even after that. This time, we will take her consent in writing."

I agreed with my wife's practical decision and moved forward. I changed the actor and location and reshot the episode. Amidst whispers of unfeasible demands and spiralling costs, a chorus of voices encouraged me to persevere, to see the project through despite the looming financial disaster. I managed to finish three episodes. Despite having written consents and agreements in place, her demands seemed endless. They evolved into trivialities like changing the curtain colour, inserting reaction shots by repeating them three times with jerky camera movements, shooting recaps in a different manner rather than using shots from the episode. She even questioned the expertise of the cameraman on lighting. The ultimate eruption of my patience happened when she recommended handing over the project to a director and production house of her choice. My realisation of sacrificing my creative integrity at the altar of foolish whimsical demands was a price too steep to pay. It was the arrogance speaking aloud because of her position. She had no clue what would happen to her if she stepped down from the chair.

Feeling the weight of her manipulative tactics, I made the bold choice to exit the project. It was apparent that she had been anticipating this very moment. I saw through her plan to pass the project to her preferred director. In an attempt to intimidate me, she wielded my signed contract as leverage, proclaiming that the concept now belonged to them. Fortunately, my lawyer friend swiftly intervened, enlightening her on copyright laws and threatening a counter-case against the channel if she proceeded. Initially, she scoffed at me, underestimating my knowledge of the influence held by the most successful channels in the industry.

Building on the drama from the previous episode with Avinash Chowgule, I had learned a harsh lesson. Armed with a plethora of evidence gathered over time that was sufficient to prove her wrongdoing, I confronted the situation head-on. The CEO of the channel, having grasped the depth of my desperation and the gravity of the evidence presented, took decisive action. In a dramatic turn of events, the lady executive found herself stripped of her title as executive producer, a consequence of her actions finally catching up with her.

In a defiant stand for artistic authenticity, I severed ties with the project, bearing the weight of a substantial loss and the bitter taste of unfulfilled dreams. The journey was a tumultuous one, fraught with missteps and hard-earned lessons, yet within its crucible lay a profound truth—a filmmaker's path is not merely paved with dreams but with a profound understanding of the intricacies of the trade, a network of stalwart allies, and an unwavering resolve to navigate the tempestuous seas of creativity and commerce. The art of storytelling, I realised, is not just with fanciful dreams but with the skilful crafting of wisdom, resilience, and a steadfast commitment to one's craft.

As the years unfolded, I found myself entwined in a cycle of revision and reflection, crafting six distinct iterations of my cherished dream story. Yet, amidst the stacks of hard copies tucked away in the forgotten corners of my attic, the shadow of a television serial remained untold. The arduous path I traversed taught me a valuable truth—one that reverberates with clarity and conviction.

In visual storytelling, whether through the medium of television serials, feature films, ad films, documentaries, or corporate films, intricacies abound that demand understanding and mastery. While they dwell under the expansive umbrella of visual narratives, each genre boasts its unique essence, requiring distinct approaches and nuanced executions.

Through the crucible of experience, I gleaned that embarking on any cinematic endeavour necessitates a deep dive into the nuances of its specific genre. To helm a project with finesse and acumen, one must unravel the intricacies that shape each form of storytelling, unravelling the threads of technique, narrative structure, and audience engagement that define its essence. Only by embracing the intrinsic differences and nuances of each genre can one aspire to craft a tale that resonates with authenticity and captivates hearts in its own right.

With the project failing to materialise, the idea of embarking on another television serial venture never crossed my mind despite being brimming with creative concepts. However, this experience served as a profound education in the realm of production, equipping me with invaluable insights that proved beneficial during my freelancing endeavours. Through this journey, I forged meaningful friendships with individuals like Pravin Wankhede, Pramod Powar, Sham Mhaskar, Chintamani Shivdikar, Girish Joshi alias Gundi, Sandip Inamke whose bond with me remains steadfast to this day.

As I close this chapter of reflections and revelations, the resounding truth emerges like a clarion call in the night - dream big, but always dream with a purpose of living. Through the tapestries of experience and the trials of those before me, I grasp the essence of this poignant lesson.

To dream big is to reach beyond the limits of the possible, to glimpse the stars in the boundless expanse of the sky. Yet, to dream for living is to ground those aspirations in the soil of reality, to nurture them with the waters of pragmatism and perseverance. It is in this delicate dance between aspiration and action, between ambition and acumen, that the seeds of success find fertile ground to flourish.

In the symphony of dreams that beckon to us, let us heed the whispers of wisdom and tread the path with purposeful intent. Let our visions be not just ethereal fantasies, but blueprints for a life well-lived, where each dream realised is a testament to our resilience and resourcefulness.

And so, as I turn the page to the next chapter, I carry with me this invaluable truth - to dream big is to embrace the vastness of possibility, but to dream for living is to embody the resilience and resolve needed to turn those dreams into tangible realities. In this delicate balance lies the essence of true fulfilment and the roadmap to a life lived with purpose and passion.

❖

8

MAKE HAY WHILE THE SUN SHINES

In the realm of filmmaking, a particular proverb holds poignant relevance—one that resonates deeply with those who traverse the glimmering paths of stardom. This maxim, embraced earnestly by actors in the contemporary landscape, serves as a guiding beacon in their journey: "Make hay while the sun shines." They understand all too well the fleeting nature of the spotlight, seizing every moment of newfound popularity with unwavering intent, for they are acutely aware that once the dazzle of the limelight fades, the world may swiftly turn its gaze elsewhere.

In the bustling world behind the camera, where technicians and creators toil tirelessly to sculpt visions into reality, the stakes are high, and the margin for error is razor-thin. Every day is a crucible, a test of skill and fortitude, where one misstep can cast a shadow upon hard-earned reputations. In this realm of relentless scrutiny, a modified maxim echoes through the corridors of creativity: "You make your own sun shine, to make hay."

To illuminate one's path with the radiance of ingenuity and dedication is to forge a place among the pantheon of successful filmmakers. Each ray of brilliance, each moment of inspired craftsmanship, acts as a beacon that guides one towards the pinnacle of achievement. For those behind the lens, the journey towards success is paved with unwavering commitment, perseverance, and a relentless pursuit of excellence. By kindling their own sun, they illuminate the way forward, carving a legacy that shines brightly amidst the constellation of cinematic luminaries.

In the enthralling world of filmmaking, where creativity reigns supreme, a successful filmmaker stands as a maestro of multiple domains, a virtuoso weaving together a symphony of skills and attributes that elevate their craft to new heights. Let's unravel the essential skills that set apart the cinematic luminaries of our time. These are very essential to make your sun shine.

First and foremost, creativity is the spark that ignites the flames of innovation in filmmaking. With an alchemist's touch, a filmmaker transforms mere ideas into dazzling spectacles, breathing life into narratives that captivate audiences worldwide. By harnessing a deep understanding of filmmaking techniques and principles, coupled with a bold and creative vision, they transcend the ordinary and redefine the art of storytelling on screen.

Visual storytelling emerges as a cornerstone skill, a magician's wand that conjures worlds and narratives into existence. Crafting each frame with intention and artistry, a good filmmaker channels the essence of a story into captivating imagery that resonates with audiences on a profound level. Every visual choice, every framing decision, becomes a brushstroke in the masterpiece of cinematic storytelling.

I remember one incident when I was shooting my film 'Sane Guruji'. It was a scene depicting the cool and calm-natured Sane Guruji deciding to join an angry farmers' agitation at the request of the strong-headed freedom fighter Senapati Bapat. I conceived this scene in a way that aimed to convey this change of attitude primarily through visuals.

Alone and contemplative, Guruji stands with his back to the camera against the tranquil backdrop of the River Bheema. Battling an internal conflict about supporting the farmers' agitation, he gazes at the cool hues of the rising moon emerging on the horizon. The gentle ripples in the river cascade a calming relief, reflecting the moon's shimmering image as if it implores him to remain true to his committed nature. Suddenly, the peaceful moment is shattered as muffled chants from an approaching crowd disrupt the silence, prompting Guruji to turn towards the sound. A harsh yellow-orange light glistens on his face, intensifying the tension. As the moon drifts out of frame, the scene transforms into a spectacle as hundreds of farmers, torches ablaze, march towards him. At the helm is Senapati Bapat, leading the determined throng towards Guruji's conflicted presence.

I envisioned an unforgettable scene, meticulously selecting a picturesque riverbank and orchestrating the timing to coincide with the majestic rise of the full moon from the opposite bank. Every minute detail, including the critical timings of the entire sequence, was carefully planned to perfection. Fuelled by optimism, I held high hopes for the success of this pivotal moment. However, as fate would have it, all my aspirations came crashing down when the person who was supposed to get the fuel to light the torches could not reach in time. Because he was unable to get the fuel in time, my art team failed to light the hundreds of torches within the allotted time frame. Because they could not light up the torches, the direction team was unable to align the extras. Mess-up on the film set starts with a small irresponsibility by someone and then it piles up into a big massive mess. Despite my unwavering determination, I couldn't halt the moon's ascent in the sky. In hindsight, the modern generation might suggest that achieving such a spectacle in post-production would have been a simple task. Yet, when circumstances conspire against you like an unyielding tide, no amount of effort can alter the course of events.

Communication skills of transcending your creative vision to your team are key to achieving the desired impact. In a bustling environment where collaboration is key, the ability to articulate a vision clearly and inspire a shared purpose among crew members is paramount. Through effective communication, a filmmaker breathes life into a unified vision, ensuring that every individual plays a vital role in bringing the story to life.

Technical prowess emerges as a superhero cape in the digital age of filmmaking, empowering filmmakers to harness the power of cutting-edge technology to manifest their creative visions. Mastery of contemporary film techniques and tools is essential, enabling filmmakers to navigate the ever-evolving landscape of cinematic innovation with finesse and expertise.

Leadership skills stand as the beacon guiding a filmmaking crew through the stormy seas of production. A confident leader steers the ship with aplomb, making decisive decisions and rallying the team towards a shared goal. In the face of challenges, a resilient leader rises to the occasion, fostering unity, solving problems, and ensuring the smooth sailing of the filmmaking voyage.

And last but not least, the hallmark of a true cinematic juggernaut lies in their ability to dance gracefully amidst the whirlwind of stress and pressure. A successful filmmaker exudes calm confidence in the face of adversity, navigating challenges with poise and grace, all while steering the ship towards the shores of cinematic brilliance. With nerves of steel and a dash of creativity, they weather the storms of production, emerging victorious and unscathed, ready to conquer new horizons in the ever-evolving world of filmmaking.

"Stress-Tolerant" is one very important aspect of a good filmmaker. A successful filmmaker can roll with the punches, be cool in a tough situation, and still make the decisions needed while under pressure. They never crumble under stress and have healthy stress-coping mechanisms in place.

In a promised to be another eventful day of filming.

"We cannot get the same student actors. Being Sunday, all those students have left for their native places," he said with a flat expression.

For a moment, I felt like punching his face, but I controlled myself. "Didn't you tell them that the shooting is incomplete and we need to shoot for one more day?"

"No! The budget given to me was for one day. How can I increase the budget to pay them without the producer's consent, who is not on the set?" He was either a moron or acting smart.

"You should have called him and spoken to him for approval on the phone." I was still controlling my outburst.

"He was not available, and then it was too late, so I thought I would call him today. I called him first thing in the morning and took his approval, but unfortunately, now the students have left." According to him, he tried his best; this mess was someone else's fault.

My main actor lashed out at him. As both of them started arguing, I retreated to a quiet corner and sat silently, reflecting on my shot division balance.

I reminisced about the extraordinary filmmaker Shaji N Karun, renowned for his composed and equanimous demeanour. Throughout my extensive career spanning over thirty years in the film industry, I have yet to encounter a filmmaker as remarkably level-headed as him. He stands out as my most revered idol in this field. His words echoed in my mind: "Mistakes are mistakes. No one commits errors intentionally. And if it is done deliberately, then it is not a mistake."

With steely determination, I took charge of the situation. Accompanied by my assistants, we scoured every house in the village, persuading individuals within my required age group to join our film project. In a swift span of about an hour and a half, we successfully gathered a sufficient number of young, eager teenagers for the shoot. Faced with my intense and brooding demeanour, no one dared to question how I planned to pull it off. Rapidly, I captured shot after shot, stretching the boundaries of my editing skills honed through countless hours in the editing rooms with masters like Sutanu Gupta, Rajkumar Hirani, and Adesh Srivastav—the esteemed editors of the film "Hero Hiralal," where I served as an assistant director. By the day's end, I had completed the shoot. As the day wrapped up, my lead actor cautiously inquired about the continuity concern, to which I simply replied with unwavering confidence, "I will."

To this day, despite numerous viewings, no one has been able to find out that the background actors change throughout the song, a testament to my ability to seamlessly manage unforeseen challenges in the midst of chaos. I consider it as Shaji Sir's blessing.

Shaji N Karun, born on 1st January 1952, is an Indian director and cinematographer of immense talent. His debut film, "Piravi" (1988), received the prestigious Caméra d'Or – Mention d'honneur at the 1989 Cannes Film Festival. Shaji N Karun served as the inaugural chairman of the Kerala State Chalachitra Academy, India's first academy for film and television, from 1998 to 2001. Renowned for his award-winning works like "Swaham" (1994), "Vanaprastham" (1999), and "Kutty Srank" (2009), he earned the National Award for Best Director for "Piravi" and two Kerala State Film Awards for Best Director for "Swaham" and "Vanaprastham." Currently, he holds the role of Chairman at the Kerala State Film Development Corporation.

Our partnership blossomed on the canvas of three films— "Ek Chadar Maili Si," "Hum Pyaar Karenge," and "Lahu Luhan." Shaji sir's decision to embark on these commercial ventures was not driven by fame or fortune but by loyalty to his dear friend, the esteemed director Sukhwant Dhadda.

When questioned by curious reporters about his decision to venture into the realm of commercial cinema, Shaji sir's response was a masterclass in humility and wisdom. With a serene demeanour that belied his towering presence, he simply stated, "I want to learn about commercial cinema" — a testament to his unwavering quest for knowledge and artistic growth.

In an industry teeming with larger-than-life personalities, Shaji N. Karun stood as a gentle giant, his voice a melodic whisper that demanded the quiet attention of those within mere inches of his presence. His subtle charisma radiated a magnetic aura, drawing all towards his wisdom and grace.

During a pivotal moment on set at Film City studio, where the heat of creativity crackled in the air, a renowned stunt coordinator unleashed his grand vision in thunderous tones, outlining a handheld approach for the upcoming fight sequence. In a stroke of quiet brilliance, Shaji sir, the Director of Photography, intervened with a touch of finesse. With a knowing smile and a nod towards his assistant, a silent directive was issued, setting in motion a delicate dance of unspoken understanding.

Approaching him as if drawn by an invisible thread, I was met with words of wisdom clothed in a whisper—"People invest millions for camera stability; how can purposeful shakiness serve our vision? Let my assistant shoulder this responsibility."

Concerned about potential clashes, I hesitantly mentioned that the stunt master is known for his short temper. "Only the insecure raise their voice on sets. I'll step back for now. Let me know when it's finished," Shaji sir calmly stated before gracefully retreating towards the waiting area. As I stood there, awestruck and speechless, his figure faded into the distance, leaving a profound impact with his composed resolve in the face of brewing tension.

The stunt master was not very happy with Shaji sir's decision, but he had no option. The assistant camera person was a bit tense as he had worked with the stunt master previously and was quite aware of his derogatory remarks. The shoot started, and the unexpected happened - in between a critical shot, the magazine ran down. Obviously, it was a break in the shooting tempo. The stunt master yelled at the camera assistant very rudely.

"How can you overlook the reloading?" he uttered some bad words.

In the midst of this tumult, Shaji sir, engrossed in the sanctuary of his solitude, heard the reverberations of discord that tainted the atmosphere. With a swift yet purposeful motion, he rose from his repose, a figure poised with quiet authority amidst the clamour. His request, delivered with a calm conviction that belied its weight, pierced the cacophony with a clarity that demanded attention and respect.

"Ask your stunt coordinator to humble himself before my assistant," his words hung in the air like a taut wire, tension crackling beneath the surface.

"Ensure he understands that mistakes are not deliberate choices. Intentional actions don't qualify as mistakes; they are something else entirely. Once this distinction is clear, we can proceed with the shoot."

The silence that followed was deafening, a pregnant pause pregnant with unspoken expectations and the promise of resolution. In that suspended moment, Shaji sir's unwavering resolve cut through the storm, a beacon of integrity and grace in the face of adversity, a silent testament to the transformative power of quiet strength amidst the chaos of artistic creation.

Of course, the stunt master realised his mistake, apologised, and shooting resumed smoothly.

I strongly believe that a senior team member should essentially take care of their subordinates for several important reasons.

Firstly, mentoring and guiding his subordinates is a key aspect of his role. Drawing from his experience and knowledge, he can offer valuable advice, help them overcome challenges, and support their professional development.

Moreover, fostering a sense of team cohesion is crucial. By looking out for their team members, he can create a supportive environment where everyone feels valued and motivated to work towards our common goals. This teamwork is essential for achieving success as a collective unit.

Furthermore, he should understand the importance of providing opportunities for his subordinates' growth. By offering feedback, guidance, and pathways for career advancement, he can empower them to reach their full potential and further their professional skills.

Additionally, showing care and support for his subordinates contributes to a positive work culture. When team members feel appreciated and acknowledged, they are more likely to be satisfied in their roles and stay with the organisation in the long term.

Ultimately, taking care of his subordinates is not just about individual relationships; it's about driving the success of the entire team and organisation. By fostering a supportive and nurturing environment, he can help his team thrive, achieve their collective goals, and contribute to the overall success of the organisation.

A hallmark of a great director or team leader is their flexible attitude. They remain receptive to fresh ideas in their pursuit of creating the finest film. Open-minded and adaptable, they embrace suggestions, recognising that improvements can come from unexpected sources. A director understands they may not have all the answers and values the input of various professionals—actors, crew members, and collaborators. By fostering a collaborative environment, the director harnesses the collective expertise around them to shape the project into its best form.

During the filming of a Yamaha bikes commercial in India, we had the privilege of working under the direction of Joel Peissig, an accomplished American filmmaker. Joel Peissig is recognised for his contributions to Ridley Scott Associates and has been affiliated with bicoastal Notorious Pictures since 2004. His directorial prowess was also showcased at the New Directors Showcase at the Cannes Lions International Advertising Festival in 2002. Noteworthy among his achievements are the award-winning Resfest music video for Frou Frou's "Dumbing Down of Love" (2003) and the direction of Imogen Heap's Grammy-nominated single "Hide and Seek" in 2005.

As we set out to film a thrilling Yamaha bikes commercial in India, the need for a motorcycle race track became apparent. Our search led us to the only track in India, located in Coimbatore in the lively south. However, fate dealt us a tough blow as the track was closed for extensive renovations and repairs.

The agency grappled with the looming challenge of altering the backdrop of our production. Thoughts veered towards overseas locations, only to be thwarted by the constraints of our budget. A palpable sense of urgency and dilemma hung in the air, as the stakes grew higher and the pressure to adapt to unforeseen circumstances intensified.

I was working as the First Assistant Director on the Yamaha bikes commercial when a pivotal moment arose in a meeting with the agency that would leave an indelible mark on the production. As I proposed the audacious idea of relocating our shoot to Film City, the room erupted in laughter and dismissive glances. My suggestion was met with ridicule, labelled as nothing short of foolish. Amidst the sea of scepticism, a lone voice cut through the noise — Director Joel's unwavering faith in the potential of my plan.

Encouraged by his willingness to explore the unconventional, I stood emboldened, unravelling my vision before the sceptical eyes. The possibility of transformation of the helipad atop the plateau at Film City unfolded before us, offering a canvas where the boundless sky enveloped our every move. Within this awe-inspiring setting, I painted a picture of a makeshift racetrack complete with pit stops, sections for spectators, and the pulsating energy of a start and finish line. The inherent challenge of shooting at low angles and capturing close-ups sparked a sense of dynamism that promised to elevate our commercial to unprecedented heights.

Joel's approving nod resonated with a sense of camaraderie and shared belief in the vision at hand. Embarking on a meticulous scout of Film City's helipad alongside our key technicians, we ventured into uncharted territory with hearts brimming with anticipation and determination. The culmination of our creative exploration materialised into a visually stunning film that not only met but surpassed the expectations of all involved, weaving together artistry and innovation into a tapestry of cinematic excellence.

As I reflect on my journey in the world of filmmaking, one insight resonates deeply within me — the indispensable quality of a positive attitude in shaping the path to success. Throughout my experiences behind the camera, I've witnessed the transformative power of optimism in the creative process.

A positive outlook serves as a beacon of light, guiding not only our own endeavours but also inspiring those around us. It is the driving force that ignites collaboration, sparks ingenuity, and propels us forward, even in the face of adversity. Challenges that once seemed insurmountable are now viewed as opportunities for growth and innovation, all thanks to the unwavering positivity that infuses every aspect of our work.

In the tumultuous journey towards success, amidst the flickering lights of uncertainty and the shadows of doubt, we encounter crusaders—mentors, guides, and wise souls who illuminate our path with their pearls of wisdom. Like beacons in the darkness, their words of advice are not mere fleeting whispers but timeless treasures that leave an indelible mark on our souls.

These crusaders offer nuggets of insight and guidance that transcend the confines of time and space, echoing through the corridors of our minds long after they have spoken. Their words are not just advice; they are gifts of clarity, inspiration, and courage that fuel our aspirations and shape our perspectives.

Through their sage counsel, we glean lessons that transcend the boundaries of mere success and failure, delving into the realms of character, integrity, and resilience. Their words serve as compass points in the labyrinth of life, guiding us towards the true north of our aspirations and anchoring us in moments of doubt and uncertainty.

In the journey of our existence, these crusaders stand as pillars of strength and wisdom, their advice serving as touchstones that ground us in times of turmoil and tribulation. Their impact is not measured in fleeting moments but in the lasting imprint they leave upon our hearts and minds—a legacy of guidance and grace that accompanies us on our quest for greatness.

I recall a pivotal figure in my journey, Bikas Ganguli, whom I crossed paths with during my sojourn at Ravindra Natya Mandir. This decisive encounter unfolded against the backdrop of a state drama competition in Maharashtra, where my triumph as the best actor and best director in 1978 bestowed upon me the honour of a one-month training programme in Mumbai, sponsored by the Maharashtra state government.

Amidst the hallowed halls of the auditorium, I first encountered Ganguli, an enigmatic presence serving as the stage lights supervisor. His silent yet profound presence added a layer of depth to the vibrant tapestry of Ravindra Natya Mandir, infusing the atmosphere with a sense of dedication and artistry that resonated with my own artistic journey. The bonds forged amidst the glow of the stage lights would set the stage for a transformational chapter in my artistic evolution.

Our paths crossed once again in 1980, as I ventured to Mumbai in pursuit of my dreams, my compass guided by fate to the illustrious grounds of Ravindra Natya Mandir. It was through the benevolent gesture of Dr Vishwas Mehendale that I found refuge within the hallowed precincts of this esteemed institution, where the echoes of artistry and passion resonated through every corridor and crevice.

Under the cloak of a quiet night, a poignant encounter unfolded as Bikas Ganguli approached me with a silent plea, a shadow of vulnerability etched upon his weathered features. Unspoken words lingered in the air, veiled by the unspoken truth of his struggles with alcohol, a silent narrative known to all who crossed his path. In a gesture of empathy, I led him away into the sombre night, away from the watchful eyes of the premises that forbade his solace.

As we traversed the hushed streets, Ganguli's words pierced the silence like a whispered confession, his request for the simple solace of local spirits revealing a yearning for the familiar embrace of the ordinary. A nearby wine shop bore witness to our clandestine pilgrimage, where the echoes of bygone tales mingled with the aroma of the earthly elixirs that awaited us.

Guided by the understanding gaze of a sympathetic bar owner, we nestled into a serene alcove of the dimly lit establishment, cocooned in the ephemeral sanctuary of shared solace. Amidst the clinking of glasses and the murmurs of quietude, our voices transcended the barriers of conventions.

"Why did you come to Mumbai?" was Ganguli's straightforward question to me while filling his glass.

"Why did you come to Mumbai? I've heard that you were with Subrata Mitra," I asked, countering with a question.

"Do you know about Subrato da?" Bikas was a bit surprised to hear his name from a young lad like me.

"Of course, I've read about him. He was Satyajit Ray's cameraman for some time. I've also read that he was the pioneer of bounce lighting in the world. The only Indian cinematographer known to the world for bounce lighting."

Bikas could feel the pride of being Indian in my words.

"So, you've come here to become a cinematographer?" Bikas asked me, gulping his super large peg and filling the glass once again.

"I want to be an actor and director, not a cinematographer."

"My son, take one free piece of advice from me. Listen to this weary traveller's tale of woe. This city, this shimmering mirage of dreams, beckons all like moths to a flame—enticing, alluring, consuming. It offers passage with ease, but the path to permanence is fraught with shadows and thorns. We, the lost souls adrift in this sea of neon lights, flock in droves to grasp at this illusive dream.

Among the multitude that converge, only a rare few ascend to the giddy heights of success, leaving the rest of us to flounder in the depths of despair. We, the forgotten, the forsaken, succumb to the siren call of failure, drowning in the relentless waves of depression. But heed my words, my son—despite the tumultuous currents, keep treading water, keep circling the whirlpool of cinema. Strive with all your might, cling to the fraying threads of hope. Do anything and everything possible but be in the vicious world of cinema, for perhaps one day, a helping hand will emerge from the shadows to guide you to safer shores. Once you are out for some time, you are out forever."

These haunting words have lingered in the recesses of my mind, shaping my journey through the labyrinth of the entertainment industry. Since that fateful encounter, I have shed the cloak of shame and embraced a multitude of roles that tether me to this enigmatic world. I have traversed the diverse landscapes of this industry, donning the hats of a production person, assistant to editors, dubbing artist, set designer, prop master, scriptwriter, location manager, production manager, location scout, assistant director, and event manager.

I have even delved into the realms of creativity as a music composer, shared my knowledge through seminars for media students, and nurtured budding talents through theatre workshops. I have lent my voice to radio spots, dabbled in interior designing, and even managed the cash counter at a local bar and restaurant. Was it a mistake to become a jack of all trades, you may ask? Nay, I believe it was a quest to kindle my own sun and garner the golden grains of experience along the way.

In the course of life, it is inevitable that mistakes will be made. As humans, we are bound to err, and these errors can sometimes cast long shadows over our lives. Neglecting one's health and fitness is among the grave oversights that can come back to haunt us. Recently, I found myself grappling with a serious illness as a consequence of disregarding this vital aspect of my well-being. However, through the grace of God and the unwavering support of my beloved family, I was able to emerge from this challenging period, albeit stronger and more appreciative of the importance of health.

One significant lesson I gleaned during this profound experience is the selective nature of sharing one's struggles with friends and colleagues. Contrary to conventional beliefs, I have come to realise that expecting support or understanding from them can often lead to disappointment. Many may initially lend a sympathetic ear, but as soon as one's well-being is compromised, their readiness to provide assistance diminishes.

The underlying fear of potential liabilities often overshadows their willingness to extend genuine support, leading to isolation during times of vulnerability. It's a harsh reality that once you are side-lined, reintegration into the social or professional sphere becomes an arduous task, echoing Ganguli's poignant words, "Once you are out for some time, you are out forever." Remember, it's essential to prioritise self-care and cherish the unconditional support of those closest to you, as they are the true pillars of strength during life's trials.

❖

9

SUCCESSFUL OR UNSUCCESSFUL

After shuffling through the pages of all my previous chapters, you may ask me why I call myself 'Unsuccessful'.

Normally, success can be defined as the achievement of one's goals, aspirations, or desired outcomes, leading to personal fulfilment, satisfaction, and a sense of accomplishment.

The elusive concept of success for me is like a shimmering mirage on life's horizon. It beckons each of us with its seductive allure, promising fulfilment, prosperity, and recognition. Yet, as we embark on our individual quests to unravel its enigmatic essence, we find ourselves interwoven in a maze of perceptions, values, and personal triumphs that redefine and illuminate the true essence of what it means to achieve success.

As a filmmaker, my journey has been a mosaic designed with practical experiences gathered from the diverse realms of filmmaking. I thrived on this practical knowledge, evolving into a jack-of-all-trades figure along the way. Embracing this truth without regret, I liken the filmmaker's odyssey to navigating the towering mountains. The journey commences with a clear view of the mountaintop, only for each conquest to reveal another peak lying beyond, shrouded in similar twists and turns.

Driven by the vision of my ultimate goal, I traversed an array of roads bearing no signposts, each pathway leading to destinations unknown. Constantly envisioning the pinnacle of success, I found myself at an unexpected crossroads, compelled to pause and explore these uncharted territories. In the pursuit of uncovering these unforeseen treasures, vital time slipped away, time that I now perceive as essential for vaulting towards my sought-after goal.

Through this dramatic narrative of insights discovered amid the labyrinth of filmmaking, I learned that the true essence of the journey lies not solely in reaching the mountaintop but in embracing the endless quest for new peaks, valleys, and uncharted territories that define the ever-evolving path towards realising one's visionary aspirations.

Success is a multifaceted and deeply personal concept that transcends mere material wealth or accolades. It encompasses the fulfilment of one's aspirations and goals, the cultivation of strong relationships, the ability to overcome challenges and adversity, and the feeling of contentment and purpose in one's endeavours. Ultimately, success is about achieving a state of balance, happiness, and fulfilment in both professional and personal spheres of life.

This narrative attempt is far from a mere biography; it is a candid chronicle of my relentless quest for success in the realm of filmmaking. Much like paving a road, my intention is that this book should serve as a map of caution signs, guiding lights, and detours erected along the path of success. It is my humble attempt to distil the essence of my missteps into a guiding torch, illuminating the pitfalls and triumphs that delineate the landscape of a budding filmmaker's journey. Through this odyssey of introspection and revelation, I aspire to offer an insight into the lessons learned, serving as a guiding light for aspiring filmmakers on their own winding paths to cinematic glory.

In the dynamic realm of filmmaking, where uncertainty looms large and obstacles lurk at every turn, I am just one among many who have traversed a path rife with ups and downs. Unpredictability and trials of the industry, I acknowledge that my journey is just one among the countless tales of hardship and perseverance. Others may have faced challenges that are even more daunting and compelling than mine. Yet, with the wisdom gained through actual personal experience and reflection, I have come to the realisation that each filmmaker's story is unique and layered with its own complexities, offering insights and lessons that shape their individual odyssey in the world of cinema.

The act of recognising one's own flaws and mistakes is a profound process that requires introspection, humility, and a willingness to grow. It involves a deep level of self-awareness to acknowledge areas where improvement is needed, as well as the courage to confront past mistakes with honesty and openness. By embracing our imperfections and understanding that mistakes are valuable opportunities for learning and growth, we pave the way for personal development and self-improvement. This journey of self-discovery and acceptance allows us to cultivate empathy, resilience, and a deeper understanding of ourselves and others. It is through this continuous process of reflection and self-correction that we evolve, mature, and ultimately strive towards becoming the best versions of ourselves.

For me, success is having a positive attitude in the world around us. A positive attitude is not just a luxury but a necessity. It fuels our creativity, empowers us to navigate uncharted waters with grace, and cements strong bonds of camaraderie among the diverse talents that breathe life into everything we do.

Through the lens of positivity, setbacks are reframed as stepping stones, roadblocks are seen as mere detours, and every obstacle becomes a chance to showcase resilience and resourcefulness. It is this unwavering optimism that not only elevates the art we create but also enriches the journey we embark on together, fostering an environment where each frame is painted with vibrant hues of possibility and promise.

On the tedious road of filmmaking, full of potholes and hurdles challenging our passion, vision, and dedication are the keys to success. The small ray of hope and positivity seamlessly binds us all in a shared pursuit of cinematic excellence. As I continue to navigate the ever-evolving landscape of storytelling, I carry with me the profound belief that a positive attitude isn't just a quality; it is the very heartbeat that propels us towards our collective dreams and aspirations.

One of the most daunting tasks that freelance filmmakers face is the arduous process of recovering wages from producers. While maintaining a positive and hopeful outlook is crucial, it often proves insufficient in the face of uncooperative producers. The challenge lies in navigating a delicate balance: demanding payment may strain the relationship, yet exercising patience may result in delayed or denied payments when they are needed most. This unfortunate reality underscores the harsh dilemma that filmmakers encounter, where securing hard-earned wages becomes a prolonged and challenging battle.

Recalling an incident with a specific producer, where I served as a Production Controller for his film funded by the Children's Film Society, brings back memories of a dear friend who had a discerning eye for cinema. This person had a deep appreciation for the subtleties of filmmaking, distinguishing between good and mediocre works with precision. I even took on an acting role in one of his debut films, solidifying our close bond.

Embracing the job with unwavering trust and faith, I spared no effort in securing government permissions from various departments without succumbing to bribery. An episode during the production stands out vividly, where we needed to purchase film stock amounting to nearly ninety thousand rupees from a film lab. On one busy day, the producer proposed issuing me a cheque in my name to enable the purchase, allowing me to withdraw cash from my personal account. Without a moment's hesitation, I accepted the cheque, withdrew the necessary funds from my personal account, and proceeded seamlessly with the shoot.

Following the completion of the shoot, when I sought my remaining compensation, the producer's response jolted me. He adamantly claimed that he owed me nothing, insisting that all dues had been settled. Displaying a bank statement reflecting the alleged payment of ninety thousand rupees via cheque, he asserted that this amount constituted my full and final remuneration. I tried to remind him about the stock purchase. He showed me the receipt of the purchase in his name. Our shared Chartered Accountant (CA) corroborated this stance, leaving me with no recourse but to part ways with good wishes, resigned to the realisation that efforts to reclaim my unpaid dues had been in vain. I am still trying to find out why he did this to me. He could have just admitted that he was short of funds and expressed his inability to pay. I would have accepted that and moved on.

The aftermath of investing my time and efforts into his film left me with a profound loss of faith and trust, even in individuals of genuine intent. The regret does not stem from the financial loss, but rather from the realisation that my valuable time and energy were squandered without recompense. This experience served as a stark reminder of the importance of discernment and boundaries in professional engagements, highlighting the critical need to safeguard one's time and resources from those who may not uphold the same principles of integrity and reciprocity.

A dialogue from the film 'Parineeta' has stayed etched in my memory: "Jahan munafa nahi, waha rukne se koi fayda nahi." (Where there is no profit, there is no benefit in stopping.)

When I say benefit, I don't merely mean monetary benefit.

A filmmaker can acquire various types of benefits from different sources in the film industry. The most important benefit is Financial Benefit. This includes remuneration, revenue from box office collections, streaming rights, DVD sales, and merchandise. Filmmakers can also benefit from funding sources such as investors, grants, sponsorships, and crowdfunding platforms. This is the most needed benefit for a filmmaker to dream further and attain recognition and reputation.

A successful film can bring recognition to a filmmaker, leading to awards, nominations, and a positive reputation in the industry. This can open doors to new opportunities and collaborations, helping him to build a strong network of collaboration.

Working in the film industry allows filmmakers to connect with industry professionals, potential collaborators, and mentors. Networking can lead to planning future projects, partnerships, and career growth for creative fulfilment. Filmmakers often derive satisfaction from bringing their creative vision to life on screen. Seeing their ideas materialise and resonate with audiences can be a rewarding experience.

Each film project offers valuable learning experiences, allowing filmmakers to develop their skills, techniques, and understanding of the filmmaking process. Each project is an opportunity for growth and improvement.

When I founded my production house, ESBE Soundvision, I ventured into the realm of advertising agencies. It was evident that in a mid-sized agency, out of several creatives, one would have the opportunity to craft a script once or twice a year. Upon approval by the client, the desire often arose for their creative vision to be executed by the industry's top filmmakers. There is nothing wrong in this as every individual will safeguard his pursuit.

While there is validity in seeking the best to bring a creative vision to life, it may not always align with budget and availability. Most of the time, the best of the lot is either expensive or very busy. In such situations, I learned the importance of considering upcoming talented filmmakers. Despite lacking an extensive portfolio, a keen eye for creativity can discern the potential and spark in emerging talent.

During my tenure as the head of the films department in advertising, I championed many upcoming directors over established names. Today, these directors have risen to become some of the country's most respected and sought-after talents.

It serves as a poignant reminder that those who show faith and trust in emerging talent are conveniently forgotten. They refuse to acknowledge them as their stepping stone. Despite the remarkable growth and success achieved by these talents, their introducer remains obscured in the shadows, forgotten and left behind.

Overall, the benefits a filmmaker can acquire from various sources are multifaceted and can contribute to their professional growth, personal satisfaction, and impact on the industry and audiences. A filmmaker who can overcome all hindrances can be called successful. Only a few, with their ability, perseverance, and to some extent luck, achieve success.

Moreover, a great filmmaker understands the importance of adaptability in time management. They are quick to adjust to unforeseen challenges or changes in the production schedule, leveraging resourcefulness to make the most of every situation. By staying organised, delegating tasks effectively, and maintaining clear communication with their team, they create an environment where everyone works cohesively towards a common goal, making the most of the time available.

In essence, a great filmmaker's ability to use time efficiently not only enhances the quality and timeliness of the final product but also fosters a culture of discipline, creativity, and collaboration within the filmmaking process. By respecting the value of time and harnessing it wisely, they set the stage for success and ensure that every moment spent on set contributes meaningfully to the cinematic masterpiece they are striving to create.

Throughout my journey towards success, I now realise the critical importance of self-promotion. As I navigated through a competitive landscape, I understood that visibility and recognition are key drivers of progress. I should have actively promoted my skills, accomplishments, and unique traits. I should have established credibility and authority in my field. This process could have helped me to build a strong personal brand, opening up new opportunities for networking and collaboration. I was unable to do it for various reasons. Was it the main hurdle in my journey to success?

In an era long past, where every aspect of filmmaking was manual labour, from the meticulous scheduling to the painstaking shot division to complicated budgeting, the weight of tradition bore down heavily upon my craft. The monotony of these manual processes, while essential, often obscured the finer details and nuances that could elevate a film from good to great. Yet, in the whirlwind of deadlines and creative fervour, these details were all too easily overlooked, lost in the shuffle of an analogue world.

It was not until later in life, well into my thirties, that I begrudgingly took my first hesitant steps into the realm of computers and digital tools. It was when WPP Group took over India's major advertising agencies that staff cuts were implemented very harshly. Senior staff were pushed to switch to computers from manual daily tasks. The transition was met with trepidation, a blend of curiosity and apprehension swirling within me. However, as I delved deeper into this new frontier, a sense of liberation blossomed within me. The once arduous tasks of scheduling, budgeting, and storyboarding now unfolded before me with newfound ease and efficiency. The boundless possibilities afforded by technology breathed new life into my work, infusing it with a vitality that had long been dormant.

Though I lamented the time lost to my aversion to change, I found solace in the wisdom that it is never too late to embark on a journey of self-improvement. The experience gained from years of physical groundwork laid a sturdy foundation upon which to build my digital prowess. The inherent adaptability that stemmed from my unconventional path allowed me to seamlessly bridge the gap between the analogue and digital realms, blending the old with the new in a harmonious dance of creativity and innovation.

And so, as I sit at the crossroads of the past and present, I am reminded that the allure of progress lies not in the destination but in the transformative journey itself. With each click of the keyboard and swipe of the screen, I embrace the evolving landscape of filmmaking with an open heart and a renewed spirit, ready to explore the limitless horizons that technology has to offer.

In the realm of filmmaking, the debate between analogue and digital approaches can be a fascinating conversation that delves into the heart of cinematic artistry.

As you delve into the contrasting worlds of analogue and digital filmmaking, you immerse yourself in the historical significance of analogue techniques, reflecting on the craftsmanship and meticulous attention to detail required in traditional filmmaking processes. In the analogue era, films were shot on film stock, which was very expensive, making it imperative to plan shots meticulously, as burning stock was not an option. With the advent of digital filming, filmmakers have adopted a more relaxed approach, knowing that any complexity can be addressed easily in post-production. As a traditional filmmaker, I find it challenging to convey to the new generation the importance of meticulous planning during shooting. Whenever I attempt to address a detail during filming, their standard response is, "Don't waste time on this; we'll handle it in post."

We will have to acknowledge the technical proficiency and artistic expression that analogue filmmaking demands. At the same time, we will have to admit that the transition to the realm of digital filmmaking, highlighting the technological advancements, has revolutionised the industry.

Most importantly, all this needs to happen in your life simultaneously as the world advances. Keeping yourself updated with the fast-moving cinematic world is the key to success.

My recent project during the peak of the COVID-19 pandemic has been a witness to the evolving landscape of filmmaking. Picture this: our shooting unit, encompassing over three hundred individuals, operating within a carefully crafted bubble in Pune, India. Our director, stationed in New York, orchestrating scenes from the comfort of his home, communicating instructions seamlessly to the crew through a laptop screen. Authorities from agencies in San Francisco scrutinising footage remotely and giving their approval with a mere nod. Technical experts located in Sydney, Australia, intricately refining the execution details from afar. The convergence of these global elements in real-time collaboration is a marvel, showcasing the remarkable transformation in cinematic processes compared to the traditional methods of yesteryears.

Excitement fills the air as you discuss the accessibility and cost-effectiveness of digital tools, emphasising how they have democratised filmmaking and paved the way for aspiring filmmakers to bring their visions to life. The conversation shifts to the efficiency and workflow benefits offered by digital technologies, marvelling at the real-time feedback and creative possibilities they unlock.

In discussing the academic implications of analogue and digital filmmaking, you emphasise the evolving curricula of film schools designed to equip students with the skills and knowledge necessary for success in a rapidly changing industry. Conversing about the convergence of theory and practice, you marvel at the interdisciplinary collaboration and critical analysis that digital filmmaking fosters within academic settings.

As the conversation draws to a close, you reflect on the nuanced understanding that emerges from exploring both analogue and digital methodologies. You recognise that the integration of traditional craftsmanship with cutting-edge technology offers a holistic approach to filmmaking education, empowering students to navigate the complexities of the cinematic landscape with creativity, innovation, and insight.

Navigating the delicate balance between personal and professional realms poses a significant challenge for filmmakers in their quest for success. While a fortunate few manage to strike this balance seamlessly, many of us, myself included, grapple with this intricate juggle. It's akin to the dual facets of a coin—each representing a crucial aspect of our existence. As we toss the coin of life, be it landing on heads or tails, it's imperative to accept the outcome willingly and engage in the game of life with adaptability, resilience, and a deep-seated understanding that both aspects are integral parts of our journey. I practically explored each and every aspect of filmmaking as per knowledge and understanding. To run the show of my production house, I ventured into Corporate films. Budgets were low, and creativity was limited with a fixed communication outlook, yet the pursuit was satisfying. My corporate films for Mahagenco, Scope T & M, Gokak Textile, Godrej Locks, Balaji Institute of Management Studies, and Prangan Pre-Nursery School gave me immense joy and happiness. More importantly, it taught me a lesson about effective communication with limited resources.

While the realm of professional success as a filmmaker may have eluded me, the triumphs in my personal life shine brightly. Picture this: a solitary figure arriving in Mumbai with nothing but a small suitcase brimming with hopes and dreams. Nights spent under the open sky in gardens, auditoriums, and solitary terraces, each providing a humble bed beneath the stars. Yet, against all odds, the tale unfolds to a heart-warming conclusion—a humble abode nestled with my family in the bustling heart of Mumbai, with all possible amenities needed to live a decent life in one of the most expensive cities in the world. For me, that is success.

The pinnacle of success lies in the heartfelt words of my accomplished children, who graciously acknowledge the tireless efforts I poured into providing them with a solid education and a sturdy foundation for life. Their reverberating sentiments of gratitude pierce through my soul, resonating with profound warmth and tenderness. The realisation that they are content and thriving fills me with a profound sense of fulfilment—knowing that my sacrifices have borne the sweet fruits of their happiness. Their loving encouragement to now savour moments of tranquillity and bask in the joy they have found in the world is a gift that touches the deepest recesses of my heart.

In the tapestry of my life's journey, there exists a luminous thread woven by the unwavering presence of my beloved wife, Bhagyashree, my anchor and guiding light since 1989. Our enduring bond forms the bedrock of my abundant happiness and success, a testament to the profound strength of our partnership. She has stood by me steadfastly, akin to a lighthouse guiding me through the tumultuous seas of my experiences.

I vividly recall a pivotal moment etched in the fabric of our shared history—a day when I found myself confined to the sterile confines of an intensive care unit, grappling with a grave illness of cancer that threatened to upend my existence. Swathed in uncertainty, the doctors' sombre words reverberated in the silence, casting a shadow of doubt over the unknown days ahead. It was then that Bhagyashree, my pillar of strength, entered the room, her presence a beacon of solace in the midst of despair.

Clasping my hand in hers, she spoke words of unwavering faith and belief, her gaze a pool of resolve and tenderness. "We, Me and our children, don't have any regrets. You have bestowed upon us the best of yourself, extending love and care beyond measure. I have every confidence in your indomitable spirit to overcome this trial," she uttered with a conviction that resonated deep within my soul. As she departed from my side, her words lingered, infusing my spirit with a renewed sense of purpose and determination.

Alone with my thoughts, a silent conversation unfolded between heartbeats and whispers of hope. Challenging the grim prognosis, I implored my doctor with a fervent plea for another chance at life—a fervour to play out the unfinished chapters of my journey, to fulfil the dreams that lingered as fragments of promise within my soul. The doctor's firm grip on my hand, coupled with his whispered assurance, breathed life into my resolve. "You can and you will," he affirmed a quiet promise that stirred the embers of hope and resilience within me, igniting a fierce determination to navigate the game of life with renewed vigour and purpose.

By the grace of God and well-wishers, I came out of all the illness and am back on my toes. This was like continuing my life story again. Being able to cover the extensive costs of my recovery entirely without borrowing a single penny from friends, relatives, or well-wishers was a significant relief and, to me, signifies success.

The tumultuous setback of my illness from 2016 to 2020, compounded by the financial repercussions of the COVID-19 pandemic, dealt a severe blow to my savings. Nevertheless, I persevered, ensuring that my children received the finest education from premier Indian institutions. Despite the financial challenges, I bore the expenses of their marriages with their chosen partners, all achieved without borrowing a single penny. This saga underscores a critical lesson for filmmakers: the importance of prudent saving and wise spending, skills that are paramount in navigating the unpredictable terrain of life and career in the film industry.

A poignant realisation that often emerges is the necessity to refrain from sharing personal problems with peers expecting assistance. Financial aid is typically granted based on one's repayment capacity, and seeking work assignments may yield slim chances. While sympathetic advice abounds, the likelihood of receiving tangible help is scarce. This thought underscores the importance of self-reliance and prudence, highlighting the sobering truth that genuine support is seldom extended by those around us in times of need.

After relentless efforts with various acquaintances and production entities proved fruitless, a disheartening realisation began to dawn—I felt as though my creative spark was flickering on the brink of fading away. In these moments of disillusionment, a sense of complacency crept in, accompanied by a nagging belief that luck had abandoned my side. Coupled with the advancing years, a profound sense of insignificance began to take root, leading me to question my relevance in an industry that appeared indifferent to my contributions. Amidst these disheartening instincts, there arose an urgent need for a morale boost, for someone to reignite the flickering embers of hope and inspiration within me.

It is during those moments of doubt and uncertainty that I find solace in the unwavering support of my family. Their words of reassurance echo in the depths of my soul, reminding me of the untapped potential that lies within me. My children's voices rise above the noise, urging me to cast aside my worries about financial burdens and instead focus on what truly sets my soul on fire - creative writing.

Their unwavering faith in my abilities becomes a beacon of light in the darkness, guiding me towards a path of self-discovery and empowerment. With each stroke of the pen, I feel a surge of passion and purpose coursing through me, igniting a spark that had lain dormant for far too long.

And then, amidst this sea of encouragement and love, enters the most precious gift of all - my little grandson. His tiny feet, his babbling words, his innocent actions - they breathe new life into my being. In his presence, I find a renewed sense of hope and optimism, a reminder of the beauty and joy that life has to offer.

As I embark on this journey of creative self-expression, I vow to honour the unwavering faith that my family has placed in me. This book is not just a collection of words; it is a testament to my resilience, my creativity, and my unwavering spirit. May its pages resonate with readers, stirring their hearts and minds, and igniting a flame of inspiration within them.

My greatest motivation lies in the art of self-challenge. Life, to me, is akin to a perpetual university education—one I never had the privilege to experience. Each day unfolds as a new chapter in my quest for knowledge and growth, where the lessons learned are as diverse as they are invaluable. The thirst for learning propels me forward, guiding me towards a deeper understanding of myself and the world around me. With each challenge embraced and every hurdle surmounted, I uncover the boundless potential that resides within me. For, in this journey of perpetual education, I find not only wisdom and enlightenment but a profound sense of purpose and fulfilment.

So, I have started writing, not just for the sake of words on a page, but to breathe life into my deepest thoughts and emotions. With each sentence, I weave a tapestry of my innermost desires and dreams, painting a vivid picture of a life lived with purpose. This book is just the beginning - a prologue to a story yet untold, a journey of self-discovery and enlightenment. And as I pen down these final words, I do so with a heart full of gratitude, a soul brimming with passion, and a mind teeming with endless possibilities.

About the Author

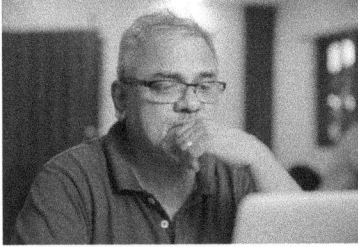

With a distinguished career spanning over three decades, the author has established himself as a powerhouse in the realms of entertainment and communication. Armed with a solid foundation in Mechanical Engineering, he embarked on a journey in the entertainment industry in 1985, donning various hats as a content writer, producer, and director.

His pursuit of excellence led him to undergo specialised training in acting, direction, lighting, and set design under the guidance of esteemed mentors such as Prof. Kamlakar Sontakke, Smt. Vijaya Mehta, Shree Jaidev Hattangdi, Shree Shambhu Mitra, Shree Damu Kenkre, Shree Badal Sorkar, Shree Madhav Vatve, and Shree Girish Karnad.

His early years were marked by a string of accolades and awards as Best Director, Actor, Set Designer, and Lighting Designer in Maharashtra state drama competitions. This paved the way for him to join the film industry as an assistant director.

Transitioning to the advertising media industry in the late 1980s, he served as an Executive Producer at Tempest Films Pvt. Ltd. and subsequently held leadership roles at Triton Communications and Contract Advertising India Ltd.

Over the years, he spearheaded campaigns for esteemed brands, including Bajaj, Cadbury, Park Davis, Shaw Wallace, Heinz India Ltd., Warner Lambert, Bharat Petroleum, Unilever India, ICICI, and HDFC Bank, leaving an indelible mark on the industry.

Since the turn of the millennium, he has continued to make waves as a producer and director, collaborating with premier production houses such as India Take One, Stratum Films, and Blank Slate Ad Com Pvt. Ltd. With a portfolio boasting over 50 communication films for global brands like LG, Sunsilk, Nike, and Samsung, he has demonstrated an unwavering commitment to excellence and innovation.

His expertise has been sought after by some of the world's most distinguished directors, with whom he had the privilege to work as a First Assistant Director.

Francois Rousselet (Paris), A G Rojas (LA), Jeff Zwart (LA), Jean Cloud Thibaut (Paris), Tarsem (UK), Garth Devis (Melbourne), Tom Kuntz (US), Samuel Buyer (US), Brian Buckley (LA), David Denneen (Australia), Ashutosh Govarikar (India), Alma Harel (LA), Paul Street (US), Bartek Cierlica (Poland), Kuba Michalczuk (Denmark), Sara Marandi (NY), Samir Malal (Toronto), David Gorden Green (LA), Daniel Wolf (UK), Paul Mitchell (LA), Harmony Korine (SF), Christopher Riggert (Sydney), Todd Mueller (NY), Mike Miller (LA), Armando Boe (Argentina), Gregor Jorden (Australia), Joel Peissig (US), Alessandra Pescetta (Milan).

His collaborations with these renowned directors have enriched his creative vision and expanded his horizons on the global stage.

In 2005, he scripted and directed the groundbreaking Marathi film "Sane Guruji," which garnered critical acclaim and multiple nominations at the Zee Cine Awards. Selected for prestigious international film festivals including MAMI and Pune International Film Festival, the film solidified his reputation as a visionary filmmaker.

Beyond his creative pursuits, he has deeply invested in nurturing talent and shaping the future of the entertainment industry. He has designed academic courses in Entertainment Technology in collaboration with institutions like Symbiosis Institute and conducted workshops for aspiring filmmakers and communication professionals at Rizvi College of Architecture, Rachana Sansad's Academy of Architecture, Somaya Media Institute, Kirti College, and L.S. Raheja School of Art.

He was honoured as a jury member for the Maharashtra State Film Festival in the years 2004, 2006, and 2007.

He was also involved in set construction and backstage management for West End London productions like Mousetrap, Jeeves & Wooster, and Broadway's Million Dollar Quartet for their India tour.

SANDEEP SHRIDHAR KASHYAP

A-2, Shefali, Mahim Makarand CHSL,
Veer Savarkar Marg, Mahim (W), Mumbai - 400016.

Email: meetskashyap@gmail.com, Tel: +91 22 9821012621

9 788119 510337